Trinity's Story:
The Trifling Series 2
By
London Starr

DEDICATION

Each book I pen is dedicated to anyone who works to achieve their dreams. This one is proof that you can make yours come true... over and over again.
Happy Birthday to Diamond Wilson and Cheron Wilson.

CONTENTS

ACKNOWLEDGMENTS

This publication is another accomplishment that will span time long after I'm gone, thanks to the people who support me in making my dreams come true. You know who you are readers, family, friends, and those that just mention me as an author to others. I love you all from the bottom of my heart. Thank you so much.

CHAPTER 1

Aruba's a beautiful, mesmerizing place with its white secluded beaches and breezes trespassing over the land, keeping the temperature at a pleasant eighty degrees during midday in June. The melodic lyrics to Sevyn Streeter's *It Won't Stop* drifts across the deck of a modern home on Eagle beach where I sit, looking out toward the Caribbean Sea. The picturesque location and its atmosphere aren't holding my attention though. The two standing on the beach holding each other between the sea and the house are.

One of my best childhood friends, the most troubled of us three, is seizing the love of her life with both hands. I mean she's literally got both hands tightly gripping his waist, balancing her weight thrown off kilter by their baby that's a month way from being born. Even her lips seem to be wrapped securely around his, but I guess her lips would be since they haven't touched his in eight months. However, that's nothing compared to the eight *years*, his wife's murder, and unborn child it took for Milani Elliot and Rhys Malone to realize how much they love each other and to get their shit together.

The only thing more beautiful than Aruba is Milani finally finding peace, a good place, and true happiness in her life along with the man that she's always wanted to share it all with. After all the storms she's been through while getting chewed up and spit out by life since fourteen, she deserves everything good that she's finding right now. What's odd about the situation is that the most troubled of my friends is giving me, the one that's usually the most stable of us, hope for my own four-year relationship suddenly gone rocky with my ex-fiancé but current boyfriend, Travis Diamond.

No one attending Milani's baby shower on the deck of her beach house, which she's been residing in for the last eight months while hoping to get over Rhys while he came to terms with the sudden loss of his wife, knows that my relationship is on the skids. I don't want to tell them either, because I don't have a valid reason for why I and Travis are suddenly so broken. He gave me a reason of course. I'm not falling for it. Something else is keeping us from moving to the next level. I need that reason before I can move on with or without him. It's all about having closure. I'm owed that after being with him for four years.

God knows Milani's been through enough drama in the last eleven years for everyone here on the island. That includes almost being wrongfully imprisoned for the murder of Rhys' wife's. I need that shining example that she's giving me right now. I've been losing a little bit of it every day, for the last two months, as far as me and Travis is concerned. I'd rather our relationship went back to the way it used to be; when we couldn't stand to be away from one another and a weekend didn't go by without us making love. Being away from our stressful jobs in Miami is usually all the excuse we need to make use of the first bedroom we can get to. At home, it would've been whatever flat surface that was the closest and had the most space for him to plant my thick behind on before he sunk into the swollen core of me.

We've been in the guest bedroom of Milani's rental property for two days now, and Travis has yet to sink into anything besides his own agenda and ambitions. His determination to be more than the successful product of nepotism, the vice president of his father's affluent bank in Miami, is what I loved the most about him. Now, his determination is what I'm starting to hate about him.

He's always seeking new connections and investors to widen his reach for opening his own business one day instead of just working for his father. There's nothing wrong with that, until his ambitions doubled and started to tear us apart. Oh, and the damn ringing of his cell phone at all hours of the night isn't helping either, although he never goes anywhere at odd hours or comes home late. Sometimes, I suspect Travis is running an undercover kingpin operation, just like Milani's father is, or rather he was.

Robert Elliot, who goes by the nickname Bob the Builder, used to run Miami's underground from behind a legit businessman guise and a construction company, among many others companies that he owns. Everyone in Miami knows his legal businesses were fronts for the truckloads of money he made in pushing bricks of cocaine from Miami to wherever. Those bricks were usually hidden among real building bricks that were stored in Bob's warehouses when he wasn't constructing or contracted to build a new company.

Hence the name Bob the Builder that not even the finest of Miami's

Police Dept. could attach to any deaths or suspicious activity. Bob covered his ass really well during his reign in Miami, and what a fine piece of ass it is. At forty-five, he's beautiful in his ebony skin with matching eyes. His well-maintained, jet-black dreads with a sprinkle of gray at his temples almost reach to the top of the same fine piece of ass that could've been sculptured from marble. Khaki slacks are molded around the globes of it, like they've both been tailored to fit one another.

I don't have to let my eyes wander to his body standing at a gas grill in front me to know that his white Polo shirt's hugging his bulging upper arms and chest like a lover, or that the large bulge in front his khaki's zipper isn't an illusion. I found this out the hard way this morning, after I entered the spacious kitchen of Milani's beach house looking for some breakfast. I made the mistake of trying to pass between the island and Bob, who was standing at double farm sinks preparing the same food he's grilling now.

I didn't misjudge the space between his backside and the island sitting in the center of the kitchen with a Bedford countertop that looks like a child took a piece of charcoal and lightly colored across a white background. Didn't expect Bob to turn around at the exact moment I was passing by either, when I should've easily gotten between them without grazing either. I guess he didn't know that I was behind him when he turned around to grab the bottle of seasoning waiting on the island for the food. I knew he was behind me though when his front pressed into my backside. Skidding to a stop, I pressed my front to the island in hopes of getting out of his way, and apologizing profusely for being in it. He laughed, making his warm breath fan the back of my neck. The fine hair on it stood on end when his deep voice pierced right through my flesh.

4

"It's okay, Trinity."

While I'm hoping he'll go around me so I can scatter like the four winds, he places a hand on my hip, holds me in place, and reaches around me for the cylinder of seasoning. The bulge in front of his khakis becomes intimate with the slit of my ass, which is when I realize he has a bulge at all. A sudden onslaught of desire developing from his hand and his nearness slings my senses and my breath to the far reaches of the beach, and I nearly pass out right there in the kitchen. The only scattering I do is mentally, but I have enough of my faculties left to wonder why I'm suddenly attracted to Bob much more than the man I love. They're complete opposites.

Travis is a white man with a blue blood background that can be traced back to the first bank that opened in Tallahassee in 1830. There's no way in hell he'd rather sell drugs or peddle flesh, and risk his elite lifestyle and his freedom to do either. Yet, he was real eager to get to Milani's baby shower in Aruba that Bob the Builder, the former king of Miami's streets, just so happens to be throwing for his daughter, which makes me suspicious of Travis. What man wants to go to a freaking baby shower?

Not a single damn one that I know of. However, if that man wanted a connection into the underworld where fast money can make a man richer than King Midas in a month, Bob's presence is exactly where Travis, and any other up and coming kingpin, will want to be.

Of course, I know business doesn't stop for a legit entrepreneur with side illegal dealings. Bob taught me that while I was growing up with Milani. I just don't know of a banker or investor that has business to attend to after the bank's doors has closed on every single night of the week, including Sunday, unless that banker has side illegal dealings too.

For the last six months, whatever Travis' new business is, legal or otherwise, has been intruding on our home life. No matter what we're doing, eating, talking, sleeping, or just nothing since making love seems to be out of the question these days, he'll walk away to answer the phone after giving me the same lame excuse.

"It's just bank business, babe. Be right back."

I have reached my wit's end with his 'bank business', but I'm not ready to cut the ties between us… yet. Each snip will be permanent when I do, so I'm hanging in there, hoping things will return to normal or get even better than normal. I won't settle for somewhere in between what we have now and what we use to have. I've even considered adding a time limit for how long I'm going to hang in there and giving Travis an ultimatum; get your shit together or I'm gone.

However, ultimatums are the equivalent of pinning a wild animal in a corner. It'll come out fighting every time. Usually, the one doing the pinning is the one that gets hurt. The last thing I want to do is anger Travis and cause him to hurt me just for issuing the ultimatum in the first place. It's best to keep my time limit to myself, give myself the ultimatum of trying to work it out with him, or trash this relationship altogether within a reasonable time frame, and then stick to it.

I know frontwards and backwards that this is what I should do as a psychologist, so I'm trying not to resort to pinning Travis in a corner. It wouldn't even be a desperate move of a desperate woman since I've lost so much love and respect for him in the last two months. This is what a conflicted woman would do.

It isn't the rational psychologist part of me that loves him, but a real flesh and blood woman with emotions that want to be with him and not have wasted four years of her life with the wrong man. He's the right man for me. Those don't come along every day. I'm not interested in screwing half of Miami, like Milani did, or Aruba to find another one.

Don't get me wrong, I'm not dissing my girl. Just speaking the truth and she wasn't *looking* for anything while helping herself to most of the poles in Miami, married or otherwise. She was living life the best way she knew how with pain that was eating her up on the inside, but I don't view promiscuity as the answer to any of my problems. I'm not a doormat either when it comes to Travis.

If I didn't love him, I'd walk away. If I didn't think he loved me, I'd walk away. If we weren't supposed to have gotten married two months ago, I'd have already walked away, but something isn't right with us or rather Travis. I plan to find out what the hell that is before I make a decision to stay or walk away for good if that's what I have to do. Rarely do relationships ever go back to the way they were. Things get better or worse for everyone involved. I'm prepared for both when one or the other happens, and to leave quickly if things get worse between us.

I guess you've figured out by now that I don't need to hold on to Travis, but want to. I'm not all that torn up inside anymore about our relationship losing steam faster than a locomotive slowing down for its next pit stop either. Not being torn up inside worries me, because I was torn up two months ago, when he called off the wedding the night before. It took me a full thirty minutes to get Travis to tell me why.

Can you believe he didn't want to miss any opportunities that could brighten our futures more than they already are? Or that he was afraid those opportunities would come along during the month-long honeymoon trip we were supposed to take sailing the Atlantic Ocean? That's why we have technology, so I didn't believe him either.

"How much fucking stability do you need?" I screamed like a raving lunatic in the living room of our two-bedroom starter home that's already bought and paid for in both of our names, on the south side of Miami. It's stationed on a quiet street in a neighborhood constructed from old money and full of influential neighbors that are or was in power positions in Florida.

Travis tugged on his navy-blue tie with silver diamonds until it sat askew on his slim chest before he answered me on the day of our rehearsal dinner. "Enough stability so that you and our kids never want for anything, Trinity."

"Well, when is enough stability going to be enough, Travis?"

He walked toward where I was standing on the opposite side of our six-chair dining room table made of teakwood with an eight-arm crystal chandelier suspended above it. Tiny white lamp shades shielded each miniature light bulb. While waiting for him to answer to me again, I remembered when we walked through several stores looking for the right chandelier that we both could live with forever. At that very moment in time, I started to feel like shopping for that chandelier, and anything else in our home, should've been put on 'a waste of damn time' list. I was getting close to adding 'being with Travis' to it as well, at the very top of it. Suddenly, I didn't want him anywhere near me while I felt like that, and threw my hands up to warn him not to come any closer. He was in danger of me slapping the shit of him until I felt better about him wasting my damn time if he had gotten any closer.

He respectfully stopped in his tracks, after covering half the distance between us. "It'll be enough when I don't report to my father anymore, and it doesn't matter if we get married tomorrow or five years from now. We're together now, babe, and that's all that counts," he rationalized, but his words only served to make me even angrier.

"It may not matter to you when we get married, but it sure as hell matters to me!" I responded at the top of my lungs. "I don't plan on shacking up with anyone for the rest of my damn life! I was built to be a wife with kids, not a permanent girlfriend wasting the best years of my life with someone who is more concerned about the future than the present! And you sure as hell won't be finding a newer model to replace me with after my best years are gone! I promise I'll leave you first!"

Travis' pale skin seem to go completely white on his slim, deceptive frame with no muscles whatsoever on it, but he has no problems holding me in any position while slamming into me until we both climax. His blue-gray eyes widened to the size of saucers. They've always stood out from his heart-shaped face with a narrow nose sitting under a layered cut in a rich dark-brown hue. His hair's too long for the military though it's shaved low to his scalp above his ears, which are almost too large for his head. At the crown and on top of it are thick strands of hair that are just short enough to be respectable for a bank though.

I stop studying his features, which are more striking than handsome, when his thin lips thinned even more with agitation until there was just a tightly pressed outline of them. His physical reactions at my threat of leaving are why I didn't leave right then and there—I knew he had to still love me even if he didn't want to marry me anymore.

To this day, I wonder if I shouldn't have left anyway, if some answers are worth the trouble of seeking.

"Babe, I just want to make sure we lack for nothing before and after we get married. What's so wrong with that?" His softly spoken question made me rediscover my inside voice, but I was no less angry with him.

"You're an investment banker with multi-billion dollar companies ran by your father that you'll inherit one day. I'm a goddamn psychologist with my own solid practice in the heart of Miami, the capital for the mentally sick and famous in all of damn Florida. I'll never be without wealthy clients that can pay whatever I charge, and neither will you since all of your clients are wealthy too and want to be even wealthier. So I'll ask you again. How much more damn stability do you need? Better yet, don't answer that. Just admit that you don't want me anymore so I can pack my shit and leave before I waste any more time on you."

He shakes his head then swipes at his brow with a million creases in it. His long, lean fingers trembled slightly, and have found my g-spot on numerous occasions before giving me just as many orgasms.

I didn't want to give that up either, when I think about it now.

"I'll always want you, Trinity. You're my first love."

"The same first love that you don't want to stand beside at our wedding because you don't want to go on the honeymoon, like one is tied

to the other," I fired back patronizingly.

"It's not that I don't want to, Trinity. I want to give you both, and I'm not going to deny you one without the other, but I don't know when I'll have the time free to give you the other either."

"So since you don't want to give me one without the other, you're not going to give me either? Is that what you're saying?" I had never been so confused in my life, and I don't do confused, but confused was doing me right then. Before that, there was nothing and no one I couldn't figure out.

"I can't give both to you at the same time right now, babe."

"When Travis?"

"I have a lot of things in the works, and waiting on a few others to pan out, but I promise we'll do this."

"When, Travis?"

He shrugs, with his eyes dull and shoulders slumped in his navy-blue, pinstriped suit.

Needless to say, I gave up on changing his mind, and prepared myself to be completely humiliated again and again, by each of the wedding guests that I would have to call up and tell them that the ceremony had been called off. They all asked why and when were we going to get married—all reasonable questions since they'd all brought gifts already, some nonreturnable.

"We're not getting married because Travis doesn't want to marry

me anymore," I responded angrily to our guests, with Travis listening in
on each and every conversation.

Yes, I was brutally honest with each and every guest, and made
Travis stand by and listen to each and every conversation I had to have
with them. For some reason, he thought I was going to let him leave
while I humiliated myself, but I wasn't going to be humiliated *by*
myself—I wasn't the one that asked me to marry anybody.

No, I don't mince words or sugarcoat shit nor talk about you behind
your back. Your front's just fine with me. Just ask Milani, Paisley, and
my patients if you don't believe me.

Now, I'm just sticking around to see if Travis and I can gain back
what we've lost while I try to figure out why we lost it in the first place.
I'm not buying into his 'our future isn't bright enough' bullshit.
Something else drastic is going on with him, and me too by default. I can
feel it in my gut and loathe being a part of anything messy.

It's that same gut and the psychologist in me that likes to know why
people do what they do, and then I try to fix their fucked up behavior if I
can. Notice, I didn't say fix someone but their behavior. Before you get
all snippy with me, someone and their behavior isn't the same thing. You
can't fix people at the core of them. Most of us are *fixed* in our ways and
how we think before we come out of elementary school. How we act
towards other people in the outside world's another matter entirely
though. Travis' developing habit, for leading me on, needs to be fixed
and fast before he does this to someone else then gets himself hurt for
doing it.

CHAPTER 2

A hail of laughter goes up around the table where all of Milani's guests are sitting and waiting for Bob to flip the food on the grill for the last time. I'm not hungry like everyone else is, but I am wishing for this evening to be over so I can stop trying to avoid looking at Bob's front and backside. My mind keeps recalling when his front was pressed against *my* backside, and I don't want it to do that. Those thoughts are disrespectful, especially with Travis sitting right beside me. I'm not a disrespectful kind of woman, but it's getting harder and harder not to be one, when I'm unhappy with my man and Bob's physique's begging to be appreciated.

Travis suddenly reaches for the closest of my hands laying palm down on the long wooden table that seats ten, while he chats with David Stein, a private investigator sitting directly across from us on the opposite bench. It's like Travis sensed when my mind strayed from him and his behavior to another man's body, but that isn't what happened. Travis only reached for my hand when David reached for one of his date's. A gorgeous island girl in a red string bikini and white netted-covering with chocolate skin and almond-shaped eyes that have dark filling for color. She looks a lot like me.

I look sideways at Travis without turning my head, while considering depositing my hands under the round globes of my ass to keep him from touching them. Every inch of my body, which is trained to watch other's behavior and packed with a woman's intuition that notices things right when they're happening often, screams within that Travis is putting on a show.

It has to be for Milani, who's not even at the table, her father, and Paisley Booker, who's my other childhood best friend. My best friends, besides my parents and Travis, are what matters the most to me in this world. David, Jamal, Rasheed, affiliates of Milani and Bob for one reason or another, and their dates are also being entertained by Travis' fakery. Rhys will be added to that mix too, if he and Milani ever stop kissing on the beach long enough to attend the baby shower for their baby boy, Jaden.

The only man on the deck that didn't invite a date is Bob. He seems happy to be single, host of his only child's and grandchild's party, and the cook right now. Don't ask me why I'm suddenly relieved about any of that. I don't want to examine why I am, which probably makes me the only one who doesn't want to know, but I have enough shit weighing down my mind already—like how to keep Travis from touching me out of pretense.

Why reach for me now when he hasn't been doing that before we got here?

I really don't want to know that right this instance because I'll scream at him to get his shit together. It's best if I let him put on that show and not ruin Milani's baby shower/reunion with the father-to-be. Since I always go with the best, like Travis, I let him take my hand in his. I'm just not sure if he is what's best for me anymore, especially since his fingers feel ice-cold to the touch, or maybe mine do. It doesn't even matter at this point. I just want to pull away from him or him from me. Whichever one that doesn't make a scene works for me, and this would be a great time for his damn cell phone to ring.

It doesn't.

He twines our fingers together tighter instead. A cold chill sneaks down my spine in the midday heat, the kind where something feels very wrong, or someone does. I don't know which is it or what it is that's making me feel this way nor why, and I want to know badly, but can't figure it out for the life of me.

"Trinity," Bob calls out suddenly.

My head snaps up to the appealing deep cadence of his voice. Only then do I realize that I was frowning at my fingers interlocked with Travis' before I responded immediately to another man. I'm extremely glad he called to me. Yes, I recognize that isn't good, and Bob's frowning too, oddly.

"Will you go in the kitchen and bring the same seasoning to me that you saw me grab earlier? I think you'll remember which one and where it is."

I'm sure he wasn't trying to send subliminal messages reminding me of what all he grabbed earlier besides the seasoning; my awareness of him and my hip that tingles whenever my stupid mind recalls his hand on it. Well, I received those subliminal messages anyway, and my face starts to heat up with shame and relief. I could kiss Bob right now for giving me a way out of Travis' sad act of a loving boyfriend. I *won't* kiss Bob for it, but I so damn want to, and wonder if his thick lips would completely dominate mine or just lightly stroke them until I beg him to kiss me thoroughly everywhere.

Trinity, stop this right now. That's your best friend's father that you want to molest you with his mouth, and your man's sitting right beside you. Now damn it, get your shit together!

After collecting myself by pushing the image of Bob's mouth on mine away, and pulling my fingers out of Travis' grip, I clear my throat. "Sure, Mr. Elliot. Be right back, Travis."

I get up from my seat like it's suddenly grown hot. Bob cocks one of his thick and seemingly professionally-arched eyebrows. They're shaped too damn perfectly and there are no signs of a uni-brow forming anywhere on his wrinkle-free forehead. He could pass for thirty-years old easily. I realize I'm staring at him, and then look away quickly, which will make him suspicious even if me reverting back to calling him Mr. Elliot doesn't.

I haven't called him Mr. anything since I graduated from college four years ago. He'll probably want to know why I'm doing it now, after he'd politely informed me that I could use any one of his first names when I ran into him at a coffee shop. Two weeks after returning home from the University of Florida, he explained his odd request away by stating we're both adults now, which I knew already. He was an adult before I was born. I thought nothing of his request for less formality between us after that because it was fine by me. It still is, when I don't need to put as much mental distance between us to equal our age gap.

But reminding myself that he's twenty years my senior isn't helping me view him as a father figure. Not when I know he's in the right age group that has enough experience to know exactly what to do in any situation, like the ones that would occur in my bedroom or his, against a wall, on a countertop, with no problems.

Trinity, you're digressing!

And I can't seem to help it either, all because of Bob.

It takes me too damn long to circle the bench on the oak-stained deck and walk past him who's standing beside the sliding glass back doors; my destination. I do my level best not to let my eyes roam down his front, where that damn bulge in his khakis persists in making me acknowledge it, with everyone watching while I do it.

Shit! I'm staring anyway.

I finally get my eyes to look where I'm going right before I reach the back doors, or I probably would've walked forehead first into them. I slide them open and rush through them like there are hellhounds snapping at my heels. May not come back out of them with that seasoning either if I can't keep my eyes to myself around Bob... I mean Mr. Elliot.

The can-cooled interior of the kitchen does little to help my composure. Even my hands shake, and I've never been so shook in my life. This is coming from a woman that just had her wedding called off by the man she wants to spend the rest of her life with and watched her little brother die in our shared bedroom twelve years ago, so that's saying something; emotions are a bitch especially when you can't control them. I don't do out-of-control either, especially when I can't control what happens to me. Unfortunately for me, it isn't the man I love that's got my emotions running through me unchecked, and that's saying something too—I got 99 problems right now and Travis isn't one of them.

I walk across the white and black-checkered tiled floor toward the spot where I first realize Bob had an effect on me. He didn't have one in the coffee shop four years ago, and recalling that isn't helping my composure either. It just makes me wonder why he'd snagged my attention in one place and not the other, and it's confusing. I'm confused enough, but the seasoning's sitting right there on the island. I agreed to grab it, so I do it quickly. Whirling around, intending to get out of this space packed with reminders of the first time my emotions went out of sync, I collide with a rock-hard chest sheathed in a white Polo shirt.

Encased in it are arms that rise up. Hands on the end of those arms seize my hips, steadying me physically. Emotionally, I'm now worse off than what I was. Razor-edged desire is streaking through me and my core temperature is on the rise. I back out of the hands' reach in a hurry until I stand in the very spot where Bob first made me conscious of his effect on my senses. I reach for then grip the countertop with my free hand tightly, and look up at him who's standing a whole head taller than my five feet five-inch frame. The rest of my senses leave me behind, just when I need them the most to be able to act accordingly.

"Uh… sorry, Mr. Elliot, I didn't… um… see you there," I stammer.

He arches an eyebrow again. I resist the urge to step forward to unarch it with a trembling fingertip that won't stop at touching him there. Grip the island and the bottle of seasoning a little tighter instead.

"If I didn't know better, Trinity, I'd say you're afraid of me, but I don't know why since you've known me most of your life."

I'm not afraid of him, know that he's not a serial killer, and trying not to forget that this is my girl's father. He's also not on the menu for sex. I'm not sure how Milani would feel about it if I ordered him up. Don't want to find out how she would feel about it the hard way either. Things could go either way with Milani. She wouldn't care or she'd try to scalp me. The girl's violent and has only two mood swings; back and forth.

"I'm not afraid of you, Mr. Elliot." Quite the opposite in fact, I still prefer to get a little closer to him, which is why I take another step back.

His eyes drop to my retreating feet until they stop moving. "I would hope not because I'd never hurt you. You do know that right, Trinity?"

His stare drifts slowly back up my body to my face, affecting the state of my breasts. My nipples, if you need me to be more precise. They harden. I curse. He crosses his arms over his chest, making his pecs expand under his shirt. More heat rises inside me. Moisture floods the tiny excuse for black lace panties under my very thin floral sarong that's held up by a loop of material around my neck. It's meant to keep me comfortable in the midday heat. It's not helping one damn bit with the heat coming from within though.

He cocks his head to the side. "Trinity, you do know that, right?"

Will you please act accordingly now, nut?

"Yes… I do, Mr. Elliot."

He frowns. "Then why am I Mr. Elliot again? I thought we agreed that you didn't have to call me that anymore. It makes me feel old now that you, Milani, and Paisley are grown up. I don't want to feel old."

Things would be so much better for me if he at least looked old and feeble with a hunchback and a walker to complete the picture. Hell, I would settle for him sounding old and insecure in a soft pitiful tone of voice to go with his demand. Well, all I'm getting is his demand cloaked in a low raspy-edged lilt meant to strip a woman of her resistance, and then she'll strip for him. Since he has no clue what he's doing to me just by being in the vicinity either, I have the burden of making sure he doesn't ever find out.

I wonder how long is my streak of bad luck with men going to run before I respond, "Sorry, Mr. Elliot, but it's a respect thing."

"I know you respect me, probably more than my own daughter does, and respect should be your middle name, but I've given Milani reasons not to. I haven't given you any for this sudden awkwardness between us however."

Oh, but you've given me a reason, Robert.

I can't say that without giving away my feelings. Awkward is the last thing I feel around him.

"Mr. Elliot, I have a lot of things on my mind," bursts out of me who's not especially good at lying, so I went with the truth.

One that has absolutely nothing to do with this conversation. My saving grace is he doesn't know that.

"Any of those things have to do with the wedding being called off?"

Shit, he's still standing and talking.

"Most of them," I say evasively, and I'll be better off if the cancelled wedding was the source of *all* my problems.

"You know you can talk to me about your relationship troubles?"

I would talk to him if it was just the things gone wrong with my relationship that was bothering me. But who can I turn to about the troubles that *he's* causing me?

"Yes, I know, Mr.... Bob." Switching up his names at the last second goes hand in hand with thinking it'll better if I don't give him any more reasons to feel old.

Don't want to hurt his feelings either. Maybe he'll stop scrutinizing me with his cat-like eyes that are framed in long lashes and have never missed much.

The air, already pregnant with tension, gets a little heavier and harder to inhale, as he stares at me closely anyway. I fidget under his probing gaze while taking shallow breaths, then look away before cutting my eyes right back to him. Don't want to give him a reason to think I have something to hide too.

He takes a step forward suddenly.

Shiiittt! Stand your ground, Trinity. Running will make you look like all the things you don't want to.

But I really want to run.

Just remember you're Travis' girl. That should take the edge off of your hormones.

But I really want to be Robert's girl—not Bob the Builder's or even Bob's, but the man in between those two personas.

It sinks in that I've just admitted my true feelings to myself, and becomes another problem—I didn't need to know how I truly felt about him. My eyes bug out of my head then bounce around the room, while I wonder why in the hell did those feelings came to me in the first place. Except, I know why. My own mind is doing its own thing, reporting shit I don't want to know, like why I feel this way.

Robert, the consummate businessman without a high school education, rose from the streets of Haiti as an orphan who has no idea who his family is in his native country. He made not one but two names for himself in Miami. There's something about a man pulling himself up by his boot straps, taking this world in both hands, and reshaping it into whatever he wants it to be that reels me in every time. Fish on a hook. Hell, I'll even swim to him with the hook in my mouth if he's thumbing his nose, which is wide and fits perfectly on Robert's square face by the way, at the people who don't want anyone that isn't in an elite circle to rise about the ranks of the ghetto in any country.

This man is damn near perfect. I know so much about him because of Jessica Elliot, Milani's mother and Bob's late wife. She loved to talk about him while she fed Milani, me, and Paisley as children in the kitchen of the Elliot's two-story home. Most women would've made their enormous house with fifteen rooms into a mausoleum. Declared war on anybody that walked inside with muddy shoes or came close to breaking something in it. Jessica ran her home in reverse. I never felt more comfortable anywhere than when I went to Milani's house after school.

Don't confuse me with being a gold digger or snobbish. I'm neither. Have my own bootstraps and money, but I and my younger brother didn't come from a neighborhood like Milani's and Paisley's. Taylor Moody and I wanted for a lot as children, and talked every night about our big dreams to acquire everything that we lacked when we grew up. He managed to find a job with a small store that let him bag groceries for cash under the table at eleven-years-old, intending to start saving for college and help out our parents if he could. Three months later, he was killed by a stray bullet from a drive-by that entered our bedroom window late one night.

At thirteen-years-old, I didn't know how to process Taylor's death. Couldn't seek solace from my parents since they both worked second shift jobs that barely provided us with a two-bedroom apartment in the worst part of Miami. Milani and Paisley stood by me in the only way they knew how as thirteen-year-olds themselves, until my grief lessened to unbearable. It still is.

Taylor had unbelievable inner strength for a child, like Robert, but he was denied his right to use it on his bootstraps and pull himself. I recognized this even then, when I came to firmly believed that no opportunity should ever be wasted to better your current circumstances. Ours are why Taylor's not alive today, but I don't resent my uneducated and settled parents for that.

They came from the hood, were fine with dying there, until Taylor actually did. We moved away to a much safer part of the east side with my mother's parents. My parents took turn going back to school and began lobbying for youth centers to be built throughout Miami, so they could prevent or break the hold of the streets on the people who were killing kids sleeping in their beds. Until you know or want better, you won't do better, so I don't condemn anyone for coming out of or just dealing with their situation the best way they know how.

Maybe a little judging of your coping methods will take place on my end. Okay, so I'll tell you when you're going down the wrong path, coping in the wrong way, and if you're going to get yourself hurt or killed, then give you alternate means that won't mean jail or hell for you later on. That's my job, literally, and it's better than resenting someone for doing the wrong thing and myself for not warning them of it. Sometimes, my words come out too harshly on my end too. It's always in the name of 'do better' and be safe than sorry on both ends. Taylor taught me that.

"Trinity," Bob summons me out of my thoughts.

My head snaps up to his baffled expression.

"Where did you go?" he asks concerned.

"Just thinking about my brother. You remind me of him."

Robert smiles. "Ah Taylor. He was a cool little guy, very respectful and a hard worker too. Your parents raised you two right. If he'd been giving the chance to grow up, he would've been someone to respect and fear in this world." Just like you, Robert.

A sudden unbearable pressure in my chest makes the backs of my eyes begin to burn. I experience the loss of Taylor's wasted life again. My heartbeat loses its steady rhythm. Every once in a while, his death finds my weakest spot inside then punches it, mercilessly. I never know when it's going to happen, where, or what's going to remind me of him. Always takes me awhile to get my emotions in check again afterwards.

I sit the small tube of seasoning back down on the island, cover my eyes filling up with water behind my hands. "Trinity, this is *not* the time to lose your shit. You can break down all you want when you're alone at home tomorrow."

It takes a lot to unravel my composure. Once that stray thread comes loose and is pulled on, I come apart like a sweater. I'm supposed to be a strong black woman—not crying all over the place in front of everyone, but I have yet to find a way to stop this from happening when it does.

A big presence descends on my lowered head, as if a cloud is blocking out all of the sun, just before thick arms encircle my body. A demanding hand gently pushes the top of my head under a strong chin. An Aspen scent mixed with grill-smoke assaults my senses that know who my consoler is instantly. I should back away from Robert's embrace immediately, but I don't want to—wasted opportunities and all that jazz. I can't deny myself the chance to be near him without him knowing my true feelings, while soaking up his inner strength that's drawing me to him like a magnet.

I do manage to keep my hands from going around his waist, instead covering my face. I'm not sure what'll happen if I touch him back, so I stand completely still with one of his hands splayed over my bare spine, the other on the back of my head. If I hadn't pulled my hair into a ponytail that's twisted on the top of my head in a thick knot, I wouldn't be able to feel the warmth of Robert's fingers radiating through my scalp and backbone, soothing me.

A knife-like craving to impale myself on the large bulge in front of Robert's khakis wouldn't be spiking in the very center of me either. It's takes a matter of seconds for my mounting misery to subside so my center can throb cruelly in peace, which it shouldn't be doing. I groan into my hands.

"Shit, I'm so sorry, Robert."

It's frustrating to have no control over what my body does around him now that I'm aware of him, which puts our family-friend bond and my reputation for having polished behavior in jeopardy, along with Robert's body. That isn't his fault, which is the reason why I'm apologizing, but I'll never be able to tell him that. He'll have to accept my apology for whatever reason he thinks it's for.

The tip of his chin slides down my cheek, setting off tiny explosions of sensation under my skin. It tickles badly. I giggle before I realize the small sound has emitted from my lips, which are now smiling behind my hands.

"Okay now, sweetheart?" he asks, with a thin string of humor threaded through his words.

I nod against his chest.

"Babe, what's wrong?" Travis asks next, from behind Robert.

Guilt and panic, both the size of boulders, collide with my abdomen, and propel me three feet back from Robert in a hurry. I swipe a lone tear from each eye before smashing them nervously between my palms. Schooled behavior makes me hide any public displays of emotions. Doesn't do anything about the fact that I've been caught in the arms of another man.

Robert's forehead scrunches up. Travis' head switches back and front from Robert to me, while a frown engulfs Travis' face, as if he suspects something suspect is going on between Robert and me. Well, he should suspect that of at least one of us. I start to wring my fingers together in front of me. Now, things are awkward and I'm actually guilty of causing it.

Normally, I don't get caught up in situations like this, which pisses me off a little bit because I *am* caught up and didn't get anything that I wanted out of Robert's touch besides comfort. I'm still caught up though, and what I was doing with Robert's still disrespectful to Travis. Then I wonder why in the hell should I care what is disrespectful to him. For the last two months, disrespect is all that I've been dealing with from him because of his damn bank business. I get a little angrier because I'm just now picking up on his disregard for my feelings; was more concerned about why he'd flipped the script on me in the first place.

Highly-educated psychologist my ass!

I'm blinded to how Travis' faults have seriously damaged our relationship. That just won't do or should've happened without me seeing it coming first. I press my clammy hands to my thighs, while Travis waits for an answer. Robert just stares at me.

"Travis, it was just one of those moments where something reminds me of Taylor, and Robert was trying to comfort me." Actually, he did comfort me, which makes me frown.

Travis' lips purse. "Damn, I'm sorry about that, Trinity. You haven't had one of those episodes since we met."

I don't find it strange that I had an episode at all. Between calling off the wedding and the drastic change in Travis, an emotional overload was bound to happen to me. Taylor's death will always be a trigger for an episode that's more like a ticking time-bomb with a long fuse always burning inside me. Only a matter of time before it reaches the dynamite. Yeah, that makes me a psychologist that needs a psychiatrist who can actually write prescriptions, but Robert managing to stop the surge of emotions in its tracks with just his touch is strange. No one has been able to do that for me, from the moment I touched Taylor's face while he laid in his bed only a few feet away from mine with a bullet in his head.

True trauma is discovering your little brother's body is growing cold beneath your fingertips because he isn't breathing and never would again because you don't know how to bring him back to life. Fresh slivers of emotion roil through me softly, and I need a moment to myself to collect myself because I sure as hell can't ask Robert to hold me again while Travis is my man.

"I need to use the bathroom," I blurt out, reach for the seasoning, snatch it off the island then step forward and shove the cylinder into Robert's stomach... make that washboard abs. At least a six pack.

I curse under my breath again. Robert's managed to divert my attention to him once again. Then I release the bottle of spices without bothering to make sure he has a good hold on it before spinning around on the heels of my pink flip flops that match the overriding color in my sarong. An opened entryway at the end of the double-sinked cabinet gets me out of the kitchen. I enter a darkened hallway. It connects to the opened living room on my right and the doorways of the master's bedroom where Milani sleeps on the first level with a half bath for the guests' convenience on my left. I'm going to neither of those places. The long staircase right in front of me is my destination.

At the top of the stairs is a brightly-lit alcove with a floor to ceiling glass view of the sky and beach, a huge potted palm tree, and three entrances to the guests' bedrooms. The one on the immediate right and a few inches from the stairway is my next stop, the en suite bathroom my last. As soon as I step over the threshold into the bedroom, I lose my shoes in the thick white carpet then dart by the king-size bed with mountains of throw pillows in summer colors on a bulky comforter that's devoid of color. I enter another darkened doorway, which is standing between a real oak armoire with a fifty-inch television and the closet with shutter doors.

Am I going to hide in the bathroom instead of congratulating my girl on getting almost everything she ever wanted in life?

Damn straight!

I need to think about when I became that girl that wants another man while trying to figure out what the hell is going on with the one that she lives with. Never mind that Robert was a father figure in my childhood who I deeply respected. I still do, I just deeply want to sleep with him too. There lays the problem.

Milani's going to have to forgive me for not being at her side right now, whenever she brings it back to the house so she can celebrate with the rest of us. I'm in no hurry for her to do that, not when I have a fresh hell opening up in my world that I need to close the gate on.

I don't bother flipping on the lights in the dark room, closing the door, or locking it behind me. Instead, I avoid stepping into the sunken tub in the middle of the floor by turning left and moving directly to the toilet hid between a short cream-colored partition and the back wall of the house painted in the same hue.

I just need to sit in the dark room and think for a minute, or a month. Several minutes pass before I figure out that I can't figure out how to stop wanting my best friend's father. Nelly and Tim McGraw shatter the silence in the house, harmonizing in their country and rap duet hit, *Over and Over Again*. That's Travis' ringtone.

CHAPTER 3

Oddly, the music keeps drifting up the stairs like Travis is either trying to decide whether he's going to answer his phone or he's making sure no one's close enough to overhear the call *before* he answers. I think this is the perfect opportunity to listen in, maybe even find out what exactly does his 'bank business' consist of.

I tiptoe over the white linoleum floor, along the mahogany countertop with his-and-her mosaic bowl sinks that sit on it instead of in it and stretches all the way from the short wall by the toilet to the doorway. I peek around the bathroom's doorway into the bedroom, making sure Travis isn't peeping around the bedroom's door looking for me in the bathroom. If he is, I'm in the right place for when our eyes meet and he scares the piss or something else out of me easily. I'm on edge already.

Sneaking around isn't a habit of mine, so you can see why I'm torn up about wanting to sleep with Milani's father while with Travis. Maybe he's sneaking around on me, and I suspect eavesdropping on his call is the only way I'll find out. Fortunately, I find no one sneaking around the bedroom, or they find me in the bathroom. I don't have to change my clothes, but I do hear when Nelly and Tim go silent. Travis starts talking in a whisper. He's hard to understand, but close enough to be heard, so he has to be standing on the staircase or at the bottom of it. I'm going to have to get closer.

I tiptoe toward the connecting entrance of the bedroom and the alcove until I can clearly understand him, then step softly between the bedroom's door and the closet. Hope I'm able to leave the dark niche before he walks into the room and realizes I was hiding and eavesdropping on his conversation.

"She's dead, Blair, and you're in the clear," he murmurs. "What's the problem?"

My eyes spread wide open, and heart does that 'lose the steady rhythm thing' again. I have to press one hand to it, the other to my mouth, hoping to stabilize one and keep from yelling out the other.

What the hell have you done, Travis?

In that moment, I permanently cut all relationship ties between us. Not trying to be an accessory after the fact to a murder, and this is the one time I think I would've been overjoyed to find out he was simply cheating on me with another woman. Even a man. Both would've been better than finding out my ex-fiancé, current boyfriend is somehow involved in a death.

"Move on to the next piece of business already, Blair. If we don't get our weight up, we flop and lose our investors, and then more than our shirts. Do you understand what that means for me and you?"

The pause in the conversation is nerve-wracking, just as much as Travis is. He's speaking in half-plain English and half code, but it doesn't take a genius to deduce that he's talking about life or death for him and his...

I don't know what Blair is yet. Wish I could hear what he's saying on the other end. It's impossible to comprehend fully why they're talking about dead people, potential dead people, and weight, like Travis is actually an undercover kingpin, from a one-sided conversation.

"You got it. Great. Now stop talking and—"

A micro-second passes before he picks up the lost thread, "You, Owen, Shane and I didn't kill anybody, and it doesn't matter if they find out it's your faces on her surveillance system now. Her murderer was caught and doing time. They don't arrest people for walking in and out of a building when it's open for business. Just don't go back in that part of town for a while."

Well, at least Travis isn't actually a murderer, but who the hell are Blair, Owen, and Shane?

Travis never introduced anyone by those names to me, and those ties between us are still clipped because he's still involved in something shady.

"You're right, because I'm not stupid enough to get caught on camera, idiot, unless I need an alibi. You should've never gone inside her store that many times anyway. That would've look suspicious to a blind man. Now—"

"Okay, you don't *ever* have to go back in that part of town then.

Does that make you feel better? Can we get to the next part of this conversation? I'm in the open here."

"Jesus Christ!" he hisses loudly. The tone of his voice is the one he uses when he's extremely angry, which isn't often.

"Didn't I just say her murder's old news and it doesn't matter if your face is in the same surveillance system that the murderer's confession is caught on too? They got who they wanted from it. If they wanted to question you, they'd have located you a lot sooner than now. But why are you worried? They think you all look alike and they're sloppy in our town. They'll just as easily pick up someone that resembles all three of you and call it a day *if* they were looking for you. But all three of you *are* stuck in the deal with me because they know your faces too. If I don't pay up, they'll come looking for all of us. Is that what you want?"

They? Is he talking about the cops or other criminals, or both? Well, I really hope they aren't one and the same.

I start to become less shocked about Travis' exploits and more annoyed that the details are still fuzzy to me. The few things I'm almost sure of are is the stereotype 'they all look alike' probably paints Blair, Owen, and Shane as black men, Travis' goons, and they're all involved in Travis' bank business which he seems to be calling the shots for.

"Listen, to me. Stop being a big baby. Man up and get someone flipped."

Then he exhales heavily. "No, I haven't been able to catch him alone, but I will. We don't leave until tomorrow. If I haven't gotten to him by then, then I'll fly back during the week when everyone else's gone home and catch him at his. He lives alone, so there's no one to overhear us discussing business or find it strange I'm in Aruba again since I've been here all weekend. Now stop worrying about my agenda and handle yours, which is flushing out someone that you can flip to produce our product."

There's only one person in this house that Travis would want to catch alone and discuss anything that may be illegal with, Robert.

God in heaven, don't let Robert be involved in this or about to be. He just cut criminal ties with Miami's underworld and has a fresh start with Milani who deserves it.

But what if Robert's making new ties in Aruba?

"No, you keep sweetening the pot until someone agrees on a price, hopefully below what we want to pay so we can buy more until we find a major supplier or start making our own product. For now, find someone whose business isn't doing well…" Travis trails off, like he's thinking. "…like the one over on Slyder Avenue on the east side. The old man that runs that business is close to kicking the bucket, even closer to going bankrupt. His customers have dropped off in the last few years since the big chains started competing and lowering prices, and he has no close kin to leave his business to or check up on him. We're the lien holder for his property, and he should be good and desperate by now since he's been making his mortgage payments late."

I can hear the smile in his voice; enjoying the old man's predicament. It's disturbing that Travis can bask in reaping rewards from someone else's plight in any part of town. Even less on the east side where I grew up at. Money's scarce around those parts and Travis knows this.

I realize that I don't know *this* Travis. Don't like him, and he did me a solid by calling off the wedding at the eleventh hour. I sure as hell won't be making the mistake of marrying him later. I then sigh with relief that I'm not torn up inside about the incoming end to our relationship, which is terrifying. Where did the love I have for Travis go? Why aren't I flying down the stairs to tell him to stop what he's doing before he loses everything? That's probably because I know he won't listen. May consider me a liability for overhearing, and I'm afraid he'll decide to handle me in the way criminals handle people who know too much.

"I'm dead certain he's the most inclined out of all our small business owners to snap up whatever offer you make him, or he *will* be, after I draw up fake paperwork for a balloon payment coming due on his property that I know he can't pay. I'd try to talk my father into foreclosing on the old man's business altogether, but my father wouldn't do it even if the man had missed three payments in a row. A bleeding heart that shouldn't be in business is what my father is."

"Well, the old man shouldn't be in business either if he doesn't know anything about the latest property laws, his rights as a landowner, and government grants that'll help him with his mortgage. He doesn't have the capital in his account to hire a lawyer to inform him of anything either. I think we have our target in the bag, Blair, and you need to push hard on the low end by flashing c-notes in his face every day, maybe two or three times a day. I'll bring down the proverbial Louisville slugger from the top until he comes around to our way of thinking."

Travis sounds so much like a Don at the head of a mafia organization. What he's about to do to the old man isn't that far from extortion either, since he's coercing the man to give up a product, instead of money, under the threat of losing his business. At least I haven't heard Travis instruct Blair to threaten the old man with violence, unless Travis is just keeping his nose clean and leaving that up to Blair.

I'm pretty damn sure Travis' definitely guilty of racketeering though, since he's making a problem that doesn't exist for the old man with the bank. That crime falls under the federal RICO act which will get Travis and his goons much more time than they or anyone else are willing to serve. But what kind of product are they trying to flip the old man for?

A trip to the east side and Slyder Avenue should get me that answer without even having to get out of my car, when I get back to Miami. Thank God that Mr. Diamond wasn't the one to teach his son to treat business and people as hardball, or I'd be disgusted with them both and not just his son right now. I guess it'll be my job to inform Mr. Diamond that his trifling son's using their highly regarded and established family business to start a criminal empire on the backs of his elders too. I'll have to get out of my car for that. At least Travis' father is an honest man who's thoroughly thrilled that his protégée and heir is a shoe-in for the family banking business.

I won't mention how much he loves Travis, still spoils him rotten even at twenty-seven-years-old, or that I don't look forward to breaking his bleeding heart. He gifted our house to us after our second year together. Why couldn't it have been someone else eavesdropping on Travis' phone call and got stuck with the decision to ruin the Diamond's family or not, before Travis ruins it and their business?

"As soon as he opens his door in the morning Blair, be the first person through it. Start low like you did with—"

"Don't say her damn name on the phone!" he hisses suddenly, which takes me right back into shock territory—Travis doesn't curse, unless he's more than extremely angry about something. I curse enough for the both of us.

"Say MM, or something else, but never her name. You don't know who the hell's listening in. Increase the increments by five grand every time he says no to you. Fine, I'll stop using your name too."

Who is MM?

I'm only certain they're a woman's initials. But is she the one dead already at this point or someone they've been trying to flip and failed?

"I know we doubled the price for her, but she wasn't hard up for money, and you should've never approached her in the first place, idiot. Her husband has the means to save her business or invest in it when it finally went belly up. She had no reason to cooperate with us. You're damn lucky that she didn't call the cops on you all and give us a reason to kill her. That's why you're supposed to investigate your targets before you approach them, so we don't have to become murderers. But the old man doesn't have rich connections that can save his business so he's a sure bet, and we'll be living like kings by next month if we set this monopoly up right."

"Good. Don't call me back tonight or in the morning. I need to play nice with the honoree of this party and tend to my girlfriend. She's acting funny around the same person that I need to catch alone. I intend to find out why that is. Lay low after you hip Owen and Shane—"

"Fine, I'll say 'the crew' from now on. Hip *the crew* to the new plan then lay low until morning so you don't tempt fate to throw a wrench in the works and keep you from handling business tomorrow. The faster we get the old man on board, the faster we can live like kings. You stay off of open phone lines. As a matter of fact, get some burners before you tell the crew anything. I'll meet you tomorrow at our spot with good news or no news as soon as I get off the plane and pick up my burner."

You're not the only one with news, Travis. I just don't know how I'll spring it on Milani and Robert.

A cold chill rolls down my spine, when I think about Robert getting caught up in Travis' bank business, losing his freedom or his life because of it. I'll bet my last that Travis has investors who don't work in a bank and will gladly come looking for him and his goons to relieve them of more than just their shirts if he doesn't pay up. Banks just relieve you of your shirt. Milani just fixed her estranged relationship with her father. She's better off with him in her life. I want her to stay that way, and won't even list my own selfish reasons for keeping Robert's feet flat on the ground.

The same reasons that Travis is already suspicious of, and you need to learn some control around him and fast.

"I need another lieutenant," Travis murmurs below me. "Blair's as stupid as the day is long, and I'm tired of taking his hand and walking him through everything. He's going to get us all caught or killed."

I believe Travis has terminated the conversation, and it's too late for him to switch lieutenants—they're already caught, which makes me the catcher in Travis' game of hardball with other's lives and livelihood. All I want to do is walk away from him for good, but no one else knows what he's up to. I nearly gag, when I recall I wanted to spend my life with this man and will probably have to stay with him a little longer if I want to get enough hard evidence to take his ass down before he strong-arms somebody else.

I slip from between the doors, and start to log questions in my head to ask outright or sneak around and find out for myself, while my stomach becomes queasy. This time, I think to turn the bathroom light on, close the door quietly behind me, and lock it just in case Travis comes up here looking for me. I want it to appear as if I've been in the bathroom from the time I left him in the kitchen, couldn't have overheard his plotting on the phone. He'll carry on with 'bank business' as usual. No sooner have I sat down on the toilet again, there's a soft knock at the door followed by a yell.

"Babe, are you okay?"

No, bastard, I'm not.

Yeah, no I'm not going to say that.

"I'm fine, Travis. I'll be out in a minute."

How could I have thought a man that would exploit anyone less fortunate than him was the right one for me? I want to believe that I haven't been walking around with my eyes wide shut around Travis. I think I'll be deluding myself too if I chose to believe that.

I've been seeing what I wanted to in him since we met at the bank, one of five that he'll inherit someday.

I was standing in line, waiting to put my name on the sign-in sheet for seeing someone about opening a business account and acquiring a loan for my practice. He was leaving one of several offices positioned along the outer walls that run parallel with the teller's counter. His door had vice-president stenciled on it. I was browsing the bank's open-floor plan with cherry wood curio cabinets on the edge of it.

They're placed against the short walls in between three large windows on each side of the main area and filled with pictures of the Diamond's ancestors meant to inspire this is a family-oriented business. Plaques boasting the Diamond's excellent service since the early eighteen hundreds are mounted above Victorian armchairs placed strategically around the center of the main area for the customers that need to see someone in the offices.

Travis stepped out of his, stopping just on the other side of its threshold. While adjusting the cuffs under his coat, he started to browse the bank too. I'd already noticed him who seemed to be looking for someone, how attractive he was in his Tom Ford suit in the time it took for me to turn my head to the front, as the line moved up. He was the kind of man that I wanted to marry some day; successful and self-confident. Suddenly, his eyes locked on my profile. He stared at me for all of two seconds before he walked around the ropes and signs meant to direct everyone's path to whichever person qualified to help with their financial matter.

I watched a wide smile develop on his face in my peripheral view just before he stopped beside me. "I see you made it through traffic finally. You almost missed your appointment and I almost left without seeing you. Come into my office and let's get your application filed so you can celebrate your new business opening in a few months. I know you're starving by now, and we can leave as soon as we're done with your paperwork."

I whipped my head around to stare at him like he'd grown two heads, then pointed at the registry that I was supposed to sign before I actually saw someone. Never mind the part where he thought I'd be celebrating with him. It wasn't written in stone that I was getting the loan. I was and still am black, a woman that had a college degree with ink that hadn't dried on it yet, with student loans out the wazoo from doubling my college workload so I could take classes during the summer months and graduate faster.

Travis seized my elbow and gently pulled my stiff body out of the line that would've made sure I spent the better part of my day in the bank. When I entered his office decorated in black, chrome, and glass that does look like a mausoleum dedicated to his accomplishments, I was floored and hadn't found my voice to tell him that he'd just made me cut the line. It wasn't fair to everyone that was there before me.

"Take a seat. I'll have you out of here in a few minutes so we can celebrate, and don't worry about everyone else. They'll be taken care of. I know that's what that look you're giving me right now is all about, Miss... what is your name? I'm Travis Diamond by the way." He unbuttoned his coat then sunk into his black leather chair with a high backrest and trim of burnished nail heads. A modern-day throne.

I silently admitted I was impressed, flattered while annoyed with his singling me out, and swallowed hard to moisten my mouth, while not surprised that he had singled me out. Isn't that what men do to the women they want to date? Once I was able to unstick my tongue from the roof of my mouth, I took a seat in a smaller replica of his chair.

"You don't think maybe you should've asked my name before you hijacked me from the line after announcing our date that I know nothing about? I'm Trinity Moody by the way."

He smiled, showcasing his pearly whites in a straight line, all paid for. "It's wonderful to meet you, Trinity. You're too beautiful to stand in line, and if I had asked for your name before I hijacked you then everyone else would've known you didn't have an appointment, now wouldn't they? My father will make sure they're taken care of and out of here in a reasonable time. Do you want to be here all day or maybe you didn't notice there are lots of people out there applying for loans? And I can recognize someone fresh out of college and starving for their real life to begin when I see them."

I blinked; found it hard to believe that he'd saw anything in me after sizing me up. Hell, I found me lacking back then. And he was going out of his way to cater to me. I let him, wanting to know what else he saw in me since I was nowhere near his league, dressed on a low budget in a plain white blouse and black pencil skirt worn for the benefit of whichever loan officer I saw that day. I wanted to appear business-like, but got the attention of one of the top dogs in the Miami branch instead, and I liked that he did things his way while showing some concern for what others think and want.

What I should've seen right then and there was the characteristics of a narcissist; an arrogant, manipulative liar who hides things from others and would say and do almost anything to get what he wanted from the people he was targeting. I didn't want to see that though. Wanted him to be attracted to me and infect me with his family's success or have it rub off on me—whichever came first—by simply surrounding myself with the people whose goals are similar to mine.

Approving my loan himself, giving me more than I applied for before taking me to an expensive restaurant I wouldn't have dreamed of eating at before my first year as a successful psychologist was complete, didn't encourage me to open my eyes. Now that they're wide open, I can barely stomach just thinking about looking at him or telling his father that Travis isn't what either one of us thought he was; a good man. Two months ago, some of his real colors started to show through, the disrespectful ones. When they did, I didn't acknowledge the darkness that was beginning to surround our relationship because it should've never circled it in the first place. There's nothing bright about making people into victims.

I start to wonder if I'm one of Travis' first victims, or the last, and about the purpose I'm serving him. He sure as hell can't love me if he's able to treat anyone the way he's about to do the old man. Greedy narcissists love no one but themselves. And how in the hell did he know I was just out of college?

"Okay, Trinity. I'll see you downstairs. Bob's through grilling. Do you want me to send Paisley back up to talk to you with something to eat? I know how you get real down after one of your episodes. I'd ask Milani to come up, but she's still busy getting reacquainted with her

44

baby daddy on the beach." He chuckles low in his throat at his own patronizing use of urban slang and excuse to steer clear of Milani.

He wouldn't approach her for anything anyway. She's never liked him. He and I both know it. It occurs to me that maybe she saw something in Travis that I never wanted to see the day I introduced him to her and Paisley. Whatever it is she saw, Milani wouldn't badmouth him to anyone because she wouldn't want to hurt me like that. I never asked why she dislikes him because subconsciously I knew I would've had to take my blinders off. She settled for not dealing with him in any capacity. I'll always love her for putting up with him for my sake.

For now, I won't worry her by asking what it is that she senses about him, or tell her about what his trifling ass is up to, until after she has the baby. She'll be angry with me though for making her miss the chance to solve another crime and put someone away. I think Milani has finally found her niche in life. She gets this weird smile every time we talk about how she cleared her name of Madeleine Malone's murder... whose initials happen to match MM's.

Oh damn, Travis had to be talking about Rhys' wife. Rhys is rich and could've saved Madeleine's business if it went belly up. The circumstances surrounding her murder seem to be fitting perfectly with some of the details from Travis' phone call, too perfect for him to be talking about anyone else. But what does Travis have going on that has to do with Madeleine's murder? This shit is getting too deep already, and all I've done is eavesdrop. What else will come out of Travis' mouth to tie him to another tragedy? Do I even want to know?

Hell yes, I do. I owe him big time for duping me into thinking I'd found the man that I could settle down with, give babies to. And if keeping Robert and anyone else out of harm's way means getting Travis, along with Blair, Owen, and ah… oh, Shane locked up, then so be it. Robert still needs a heads up pronto, and I'll have to stop hiding from them both in the bathroom to give him that. Maybe Robert knows Travis' goons, or of them, and can shed a little light on Travis' bank business, which I suspect has absolutely nothing to do with a bank.

"Trinity," Travis calls through door—I'd forgotten to answer his last question about Paisley.

"No, Travis. Leave everyone alone. I'm finishing up now."

"Well, in that case, I'll wait for you."

"No!" I shout then regret it—I'm supposed to be depressed and want to be around him. "Go fix us a plate before all of the food's gone. Jamal's a hog. David looks like he could eat a horse. I'm not too sure about Rasheed, but Milani can down two horses right now since she's pregnant. I have no idea where she puts all that damn food at." I hope I explained away my sudden revulsion for his company and blinded him to the drastic change in *my* behavior. Travis is used to be my everything, and he knows that too.

"What do you want on your plate?"

Your head, you trifling bastard.

Yeah, no I'm not going to say that either. "A leg quarter, potato salad, and a glass of tea please."

"Got it, babe. Hurry up. I miss you."

What the hell ever!

Apparently, the fakery isn't over.

"Okay," I respond, refusing to lie to him outright.

What I'm about to do to him under wraps will be bad enough, but he deserves it for lying since the day we met. As a matter of fact, I wouldn't be surprised if he knew who I was in the bank, and he wanted a meet and greet with Milani's father from the start. Travis would've had to stick around after our first date though, once he found out that Milani and Robert were estranged, until eight months ago when Robert whisked Milani off to Aruba. Travis finally got a chance to have that meeting with Robert when Milani called to invite us to her baby shower, which was two months ago, when Travis called off the wedding.

Eight months earlier, it was Rhys wanting a meeting with Robert, to ask about three black men that neither Milani nor Rhys knew about or of. Those men were harassing Madeleine about selling them narcotics in bulk or weight out of her pharmacy. Their offer doubled every time she said no—the same modus operandi that Travis mentioned his goons were using to flip people.

The bastard! Manipulating, trifling, no good, using, and conning... bastard!

I cover my eyes up with both hands, wish I could un-see all the things unfolding before them. Then life would return to normal for me, and I could chalk all these connections between Madeleine's murder and Travis' big dream to live like a king in Miami's underworld up to coincidence. However, all the roads leading back to him are too obvious to be ignored. Coincidence's nothing more than Karma's sister right now. Both are bitches, but neither applies here... yet. When the all chips fall down though, coincidence is what Travis will want to believe is happening too when he finds out it's me that'll give Miami Police Dept. evidence of his crimes. Then Karma will step in to ruin him, just like he's planning to do to the old man.

Maybe Coincidence and Karma will induct me in their Hall of Payback, and let me move in too when this is all over. I'll probably have to find somewhere else to start over, just like Milani did after the shit hit the fan in Miami. There's every chance that Mr. Diamond may come after me for ruining his son, just because he loves him.

I mull over telling him and anyone else besides Robert anything. Mr. Diamond will find out soon enough what his son's been up to, when Travis calls him for bail money. The less people that know about my behind-the-scenes involvement, the better.

CHAPTER 4

It takes one fake flush for the benefit of Travis if he's standing outside the door, the real washing of my hands to try and cleanse them of his touch, and a long look in the mirror for reminding myself that I can get through anything... and to prepare to leave the bathroom. When I open the door, Travis is nowhere to be seen. I push my feet back in my shoes before walking slowly back toward the deck. The back of Robert's head is the first thing I see through the sliding back doors. Right then, I know he's sitting right across from my empty seat at the table. David's now sitting at one of the heads of the table, which is where Robert should be, and David's date is now sitting at the end of my side of the table whispering to him.

Why in the hell did they all move?

I avoid looking anyone in the eye, take the scenic route to my seat, and lift one leg over the bench really slow, then the other at the same speed. Travis' and Robert's presence combined makes me more than damn anxious. It's like they already know what I know, and I have to pretend all is as it should be with the one that thinks I still love him, while hoping to get the other man alone so I can inform him that I, a trusted family friend of seventeen years, have brought Travis' con and exponential danger to his door.

I wonder again why David and his date moved to the end of the table near the trio of steps that lead to the beach in one direction, the front of the house in the other, while bowing my head to pray over the plate of food that Travis fixed for me. This prayer will have absolutely nothing to do with blessing the feast though. Why would I pray over food that I know is going to choke me whether I pray or not?

God, please guide me away from confronting the man beside me before I have every detail of his bank business on paper and in the cops' hands. I also need to be steered away from my newest obsession of having the man in front of me molest me. Amen. Oh, and I'm about to start drinking heavily. It can't be avoided with my present circumstances, so forgive me in advance for this sin, because it's going down when I find the liquor. Amen again.

When I look up, everyone at the table's staring at me, including Rhys and Milani. Her thick glossy lips smirk from the other end within her café au lait-colored complexion flooded with a glow of more than just pregnancy hormones—true happiness. "You could've warned us that you were going to say grace, T, and included us."

"Trust me, Milani, when I say grace is the…" I waver; about to reveal the true meaning of my prayer, but truth wouldn't be good for anyone at this point. "Sorry everyone, just say amen, and God and I won't trip about you not bowing your heads."

I need my prayer to reach higher than the ceiling and as many

50

cosigners as I can get to uplift it. A murmur of quiet amen's go up. Everyone begins to eat. A hand squeezes my knee suddenly, surprising the hell out of me. My leg jerk upwards out of reflex, hopefully out of the grip of a phantom hand that's molesting me.

God, you answered that prayer too swiftly.

My knee smashes into the underside of the table. It rockets upward, nearly dumping everyone's plates off the opposite end into the laps that have the misfortune of sitting on the other side of me. Everyone reaches for the porcelain plates sliding along the table's top and the rocking glasses filled with their chosen drink, before looking toward the center of the table at me, with puzzled expressions. Except Travis, who's snickering. I turn my head to glare at him while completely embarrassed about my reaction to his sudden mischievousness, which is not quite that sudden since he'd already warned me during the phone call that this was coming.

"Someone's frisky," Robert quips from around a mouthful of food.

Laughter erupts around the table. I notice a devious glint in Travis' eyes that I haven't seen in two months.

No buddy, we won't be screwing tonight.

"Stop it," I hiss.

Travis' lips curl into a small smile, then he glances at Robert from below his thin eyelashes before dropping his head toward his plate. I'm sure I wasn't supposed to notice the look that he gave Robert, and I hope to God that Travis isn't jealous and trying to prove a point; establishing who I belong to. Since I'm not stupid and know that's exactly what he's

51

doing, I decide to go to bed completely drunk and fully clothed, maybe even with my shoes on, for the remainder of my days as his girlfriend. Who wants to kiss and have sex with someone that has alcohol reeking from their pores and breath after you peel layers of material off them?

With any luck, not Travis, who shovels food that he's skewered off his chicken into his mouth. I lift my fork to stab the thigh section of mine. Succulent juices escape from the meat. My stomach whines quietly about being empty. I realize I could actually eat.

Nope, not torn up inside at all about Travis, and I guess that's a good thing considering what I'm about to do to him.

It's not so good when mental space previously occupied by him is filling up with images of Robert, who's tearing aluminum foil from around his potato with clean blunt-shaped nails on long fingers. I wonder how they'll feel when touching me inside and out.

He's still not available, Trinity.

I stuff the chicken in my mouth, smothering the curse words evoked from my inappropriate thoughts. Robert's proving to be too much of a distraction. I chump down on the meat, then chew like a horse, to drown out my own mind while surfing the table for something else to divert me from my troubles; Robert's fingers and Travis' sudden interest in me along with his shady activities. A light giggle draws my attention to the right. I turn my head away from David and his date to the opposite end where Paisley sits, with Milani on her left at the head of the table and Rasheed on her right.

Rasheed receives one of Paisley's beautiful smiles that she reserves for her favorite people. I'm surprised that she's even acknowledging him, since she's usually shy around strangers and her parents have a long list for her requirements in a man. So far, no one has managed to meet their standards *and* Paisley's. I sense she's been lonely since she took her virginity in her own hands, giving it to a boy in our eleventh-grade English class. She did it out of spite; defying her parents.

Nelson and Lily Booker were strict, make that completely damn rigid, during Paisley's upbringing, and are still determined to guide her life down a wealthy man's path. She struck back at them the only way she could at sixteen, then realized too late that she'd cut off her nose with her spite and damaged no one's face but her own gorgeous biracial one.

It's not a requirement for women to be virgins before marriage anymore. She deeply regrets sleeping with the boy. He ruined her first time. Her parents are ruining her life by trying to run it. Paisley's going to get tired of that and snap on them at some point. When she does, I'll encourage the cops to come running in a hurry.

For now, I clearly see that she's enjoying herself, and that she's loss a significant amount of weight. Her pale skin seems to stand out against the thick shoulder straps of her black one-piece bathing suit barely keeping her D cups contained and out of her plate. Rasheed's jet-black eyes shift from them to her face often. Each time he looks down, the tip of his tongue caresses the inside of his lips. Paisley either smiles or giggles when she catches his eyes south of her neck. These two will be molesting each other before the night falls. Better yet, make that before the day is over. For Paisley's sake, please let Rasheed's molesting techniques surpass the boy's that had a man's body with an eleventh grader's sexual abilities trapped inside it.

Since I'm thinking of a man's body, my eyes drift to Robert, who's currently staring at me with what seems like all the heat of the sun trapped in his gaze. My body starts to collect that heat, without my permission, in its core that begins to send echoes of sensation through my walls. It's as if it's sending a message back to Robert in Morse code. Unfortunately for my core, nobody's getting its message but me. The ripples of lust stomping through my tunnel are starting to become painful for us both.

I smile weakly at him then stab my food again, taking out my frustration, sexual and otherwise, on it. If it wasn't for Travis, I probably wouldn't be this hard up for sex, and drooling over my best friend's father.

Robert chuckles. "The chicken's already dead, Trinity."

"And she needs to be eating it, not killing it again," Travis chimes in on the conversation happening on two different unspoken wavelengths between Robert and me; his paternal and mine... don't need to be mentioned again.

Travis shoves a forkful of food from his plate in front of my mouth. My first instinct is to push his hand away, and then a second kicks in.

Play along, Trinity. You need hard evidence about his plan, remember?

I open my mouth. He fits the meat in without grazing my lips then curves his palm underneath the fork, catching the juices that'll grease my clothes and ample C-cups. I clamp down on the utensil, scraping it clean with my teeth before forcing myself to chew. Suffice it to say I don't want anything right now from my future ex, so I swallow the meat hurriedly. A lump of it sticks in my throat. I already knew the food would choke me—I just didn't know it would be Travis' that would be doing the job.

Why am I not amazed?

I try to clear my throat, while beating my chest with the side of my fist simultaneously. Robert reaches across the table and lifts the sweaty body of my glass of tea. I take it from him, gulp the beverage down in exactly seven swallows, before relieving my hand of the empty cup.

"Thank you," I say hoarsely. "Got anything stronger?"

His eyebrows shoot up to the top of his pencil-straight hairline. "What do you want to drink?"

"Not tea." Not sure what Milani has stashed in the liquor cabinet in the living room of her rental property.

Robert's fork clatters on his plate. "I'll surprise you then."

I watch him stand up, boost one muscular thigh over the bench, and then the other. I can promise you that my legs aren't muscular in the least, but they're more than capable of wrapping around Robert's waist and staying put. I find much joy in ogling his rear end, which my heels will rest on if I ever get my legs around him, on his trek to the sliding doors. He disappears into the kitchen. It's safe to say that I don't care about disrespecting Travis anymore. I'm sure he can tell too, since his eyes are currently burrowing into the side of my face.

I swivel my head to look at him innocently. If he can be conniving then pretend he's done nothing wrong, so can I. I smile then pick up my fork to attack the potato salad before depositing a clump of it into my mouth. In my peripheral, he narrows his eyes. I decide that small talk's in order before he starts wondering why I am acting like this, and then stops wondering because he's figured it out.

"Have you decided when the wedding's back on, or are we still shacking, Travis?" I ask snidely.

Being a bitch is par for the course when your man says he doesn't want to marry you the day before your wedding. Isn't that how I'm supposed to be acting anyway?

His mouth drops open, his eyes to his plate, but he won't be speculating about my odd behavior around Robert if he has to focus on reacting to me.

"Trinity, we'll talk about this when we get home," he replies dryly, already tired of the small talk and not looking at me anymore. Good.

I spew, "Fine," and mimic his tone, just to complete the starring role of pissed-off woman.

The atmosphere around the table gets eerily quiet. Robert steps through the sliding doors again, with a tumbler half-filled with two fingers of red liquid and a single ice cube in one hand, a another glass of tea in the other. He takes a look around the deck with a confused expression morphing on his face.

"What happened? I was gone only a minute." About the time it takes for someone's world to change forever.

Milani sets her fork down. "T asked Travis when he's rescheduling their wedding. He doesn't want to talk about it… right now," she reports with a little too much glee in her tone and a big grin on her face.

Robert's eyes swivel to me, along with everyone else's. Theirs don't have the same hardness that's visible in his right now.

"Are you good?" he asks with a bite to his tone.

I nod solemnly, and then drop my head down, as if it's too heavy to hold up suddenly. If I had answered Robert vocally, my tone would've had too much glee in it too. It's best to let everyone think that Travis is breaking my heart all over again, even if I don't want Robert thinking that. However, I'm not sure if I should be thinking that either. It feels more like Travis extremely disappointed me, ruined my plans for our future together.

It's a good time to realize you truly didn't love the man, isn't it, Trinity? I guess you were using him too.

At least it wasn't for or to make money. However, his station in life doesn't resemble the one I lived in on the east side that took my brother. I'm not about to give that side of town anymore lives or want to be with a man that's comfortable living there.

Robert approaches the table and sets the glasses down in front of me with a little too much force than necessary. Thumps from the glasses striking the table echo under the overhanging roof of the back porch. I snap the tumbler up with two fingers of the oblivion that I'm seeking, taking a deep sip from it. It tastes like someone dropped a basket of fruit into my mouth. I decide I like it, just before a dry fire erupts in my throat and starts to blaze all the way down my chest into the pit of my stomach. I cough until the five-alarm blaze lets up, then curse when I can speak around the simmering inferno.

"What the hell did you give me?" I ask throatily.

A quiet snort comes from Paisley's directions. Quiet giggling and outright laughter at my expense follows. Even Robert gets infected with the humor flowing freely now, and starts to smile.

"Coecoei, no chaser, and can only be bought in Aruba. I thought you'd like it since it tastes sweet but packs a hell of a punch."

"Robert, I need a chaser. I'm not that hard of a drinker," I spit, happy to have brought back the fun-filled light atmosphere that baby showers are supposed to have, after I chased it away intentionally.

"Then I'll make you a cocktail out of it later. For now, drink your tea. Our food's getting cold and I don't like cold food."

I fork more potato salad. "Milani, are you and Rhys moving back to Miami?" I ask, not for the sake of conversation, but because I really want to know what my best friend's going to do with her life beyond Rhys' reappearance in it and their baby's birth.

She shakes her head and swallows what amounts to a whole leg. "If I decide to go back to Florida, I'd probably move to one of the surrounding cities of Miami, but Miami's out."

Paisley lifts her finger, her signature way of requesting 'wait a minute', while trying to clear her mouth of baked beans and glazed ribs. "I love Aruba and everything, Milani, but we miss you. And I want to see my nephew after he's born, not hear about his milestones over the phone and then hope to get time off of work to visit him and you before months have passed in between his growth spurts. I know you have to do what's best for your family but just remember those you're leaving behind are family too and love you just as much."

Milani smiles. "I haven't nor will I ever forget about my sisters, P, and I can visit you in Miami, just not live there again."

"Good because Trinity and my nights out together aren't the same without you. It isn't fun when she focuses all of her helicopter parenting and motivational sermons on me," she quips with one of her beautiful smiles on display. Then it's gone. "You don't have to move back to Miami. Hell, I'd move away if I could, but being just a road trip away from you sounds good to me too. Just consider it and I'll help you with the move."

"You can move away from Miami too, P," I inject. "You're twenty-five, a grown woman attached at the hip to no one or anything in Miami, and don't have to marry anyone you don't want to despite what your parents want you to think. They're smothering you. You're slowly dying inside. It's starting to show on the outside. You're fading away, love, and I'd rather visit you in Aruba too than watch your light dim and you fade away to nothing. I'll even help you move away from Miami if you want me to." I prop my elbows on the table in a show of seriousness. "I'm my own boss so I don't have to okay it with anyone to do anything that helps you live the life you want."

Tears gather in her eyes, just before she covers her face with both hands. Damn it! I told you, I'm too harsh sometimes, and feel completely terrible for making her cry. I get up from my seat as Rasheed wraps a thick arm around her slight shoulders that are shaking, pulling her to him. As I get closer, I see her collar bones are jutting out even more from her skin than they were two weeks ago on our last night out. She's even slimmer than I realized and really fading away. I rush to Paisley's side then crouch between her and Rasheed, as she twists at the waist and collapses forehead first into his chest half-covered in an opened short-sleeve, casual shirt above navy-blue board shorts. I begin to pat her back, hoping to undo the damage I've done.

"Sorry, P, you know my mouth gets away from its filter sometimes."

"*Sometimes*," Milani shrieks, before succumbing to a case of the giggles.

Paisley snorts, almost inhaling the small gold cross on a thick Figaro chain around Rasheed's neck. He squints down at me. I whisper 'I'm sorry' to him, for ruining some of the time they have left, before they go home and her parents find a way to intervene in their fragile relationship. Somehow, I just don't think Rasheed's a holiday fling for Paisley.

She sits up, swiping at her eyes before smiling at me. "You didn't say anything wrong, Trinity, and not the reason I'm crying. Your mouth getting away from the filter that doesn't exist by the way is nothing new. I've just been considering the best thing for me may be to move away from Miami… and my parents. They're really pressuring me to go on more dates with the men they consider eligible bachelors. Running my life is one thing. Trying to marry me off is another and I'm tired of it, but

I don't want to hurt them. They're my parents."

"I understand that you're conflicted." I wish I was the only who felt like this. "It's hard to willingly disappoint our parents no matter what they want for us, but it's your life and you should say no, honey, if that's what's best for you. I know you don't want the guilt that'll come with hurting them, but imagine how you'll feel if you settle for a man that you don't want, for the rest of your life. If your parents really love you, they'll forgive you for disappointing them, but whatever you decide I'm here… or there to help with whatever you need. I don't just preach. I try to carry my weight in our friendship as well."

I hope I've eased her mind somewhat about the decision she has to make. Having support always takes some of the strain away. Making her parents back off will take care of most of what's left. I'm pretty sure Rasheed or the next guy she's interested in will handle any residue stress that just being alive brings, in one of the ways that a man can.

Milani reaches across the table and cups Paisley's cheek, before turning her face to hers. "You know I'll come running if you need me, and Rhys can't stay in Aruba permanently. He has a practice to run like Trinity does. I can't get on a plane now since I'm so far along, but I promise to come back to Florida and look for a place near Miami as soon as I and the baby can travel."

"You'd do that for me?" Paisley asks in a child-like voice, completely stunned and not quite able to fully mature with her parents blocking any attempts and mistakes she'll make on her rite of passage to becoming a true adult.

"I'd do anything for you, baby girl," Milani whispers, with her eyes suddenly too bright.

Robert's fork clatters on his plate again. "Okay, enough of the mushy stuff. I'm going to turn the music up louder so you three can't hear each other talk and bring the gifts out from the dining room. Trinity, you're already up, so you're drafted to help me. Why and how you and Paisley brought out a whole department store and relocated it to Aruba for Jaden, I'll never know," he grumbles while disappearing through the sliding door again.

Laughter fills the deck. I get quickly to my feet, preparing to defend Paisley and my spending on our first nephew, first born of our clique. Taking the perfect excuse I've just been given to catch Robert alone.

"Wait a minute, Robert. You don't talk about me and Paisley then walk away. That's just rude as hell," I gripe on my way into the kitchen filled with the notes of K. Michelle's *Love Em All*.

He's already rounded the island and picking up a huge box wrapped in blue and yellow teddy bears on a white background. It's one of many gifts stacked on the dining room table located on the other side of the kitchen in front of a massive bay window with an unobstructed view of the sea.

"What the hell is in this thing?" he asks grumpily.

I giggle, seeming to do that a lot around him lately. "It's a combination of playpen, stroller, and 3-piece car seat that breaks down as the baby grows up. I had to have a man lug it into the buggy, out of it into the car, to and from the plane. You got the honor of carrying it into the house when we arrived here, and you asked what was in it then too."

He grimaces at me while walking past. "I should've made Travis carry it after he took your luggage upstairs the day you got here." Robert's griping reminds me again that he needs to be informed of what else Travis was carrying when we got here.

"You said that too," I call out to his retreating form then linger around the table, gathering the smaller gifts slowly, while waiting for Robert to return.

Forever passes before he comes back. The need to speak with him has doubled in urgency, and I have gifts stacked up to my chin.

Robert finally steps beside me. "You're cheating by just grabbing the small stuff, Trinity."

I glimpse at the back doors, checking for anyone that's near them and followed him. "And you need to stay away from Travis. He's into some bad shit, trying to involve you somehow. Just say no to whatever it is."

His eyes narrow and jaw locks, as the skin on his face pulls tight. It's like he's taking on another persona; Bob the Builder. The mood in the room grows as thick as a jungle that has to be macheted to move through. I know I need to move, been in here too long, and take a step to the side of Robert.

"Explain," he demands, and grabs my elbow, stopping all forward progress, almost upsetting my towers. Robert wouldn't handle me like this. Yeah, it's definitely Bob I'm talking to, and his inner strength's suddenly showing on the outside.

"No time to—"

"*Make* time, Trinity."

"I can't. Travis' suspicious enough of me already. Later," I promise, just before I pull my elbow out of Robert's grasp.

Travis walks through the back doors with his hands buried in the pockets of his blue jeans with tiny rips down the front of them.

Oh my damn!

CHAPTER 5

"Everything alright?" he asks stiffly.

I walk towards him. Can't help peering back at Robert, whose calm, smiling version of himself looks over his shoulder at us.

"No. Trinity's trying to carry all the small gifts at one time and going to hurt something. I'm trying to stop her. She won't listen."

I'll give him this much; he's a fast thinker on his feet. I guess you would have to be to run a crime syndicate and several legal companies simultaneously. Even I'm convinced that he's telling the truth right now, impressed with the consummate liar that he is. Before you ask why I'm impressed when Travis is the same thing and I hate him for it, Robert or Bob or… whoever… is using that ability to save my ass right now. I stop in front of Travis, who's blocking the doors and giving me the once over, like there's a coating of something covering me.

"She never listens, Bob. Thinks she can do anything alone." Travis doesn't seem to be about to do anything though, as in moving to the side so I can pass.

"If I could do anything, Travis, I'd have already walked through your skinny ass and be on the other side of the door by now with these gifts. If you're not going to help me carry them, at least help yourself out of my way."

His hands dive from his pockets to grab the boxes locked to my chest by my chin and hands. His eyes capture mine then drill into them, as if he's trying to communicate visibly with me while scooping up the first three layers of boxes. I assume one of two messages could be he knows I'm onto him or that my body is tuned to another man's. It could very well be that he's trying to relay both. I hope it's neither, cock my head, and glare at him with an expression meant to fry his eyeballs and whatever part of his brain that holds information.

He smiles while catching the gifts to his abdomen with both large hands. I wait for him to turn around, then follow him to the small table sitting against the wooden railing at the back of the deck, where Milani will open gifts as Paisley hands them to her. That's the plan or rather it was. Paisley seems to be missing now, along with Rasheed of course. I guess tonight's too far away for them, and I think that she might be finding her happily ever after right along with Milani.

After Travis steps to the side, I unload my boxes on top of his haul, turn around to go back for another load, praying Robert isn't stalling and waiting for a chance to talk to me alone. That would be the worst thing to do with Travis popping up out of thin air, continuously catching us together. I don't have to look back to know Travis is trailing me. Just before I step inside the back doors, Robert passes by the island with another big package of baby outfits for winter and summer.

I sidestep, avoiding the hot grill. He avoids looking at me as he passes, but his expression holds no trace of his Bob the Builder side. My edginess wears off some. The rest of my nerves will settle when Travis isn't standing so close to me, close enough to keep both eyes on me. When Robert retraces my steps to the gift table, I retrace his to the dining room table where only a few more small gifts wait.

"I can get these, Travis. You can go eat or handle bank business or something," I mention breezily.

"I'm good. I don't mind following you around."

"Oh now you remember I exist? I'm good. Go back to your bank business... or something."

He exhales behind me. "If I didn't know better, I'd think you were trying to get rid of me, Trinity, so you and Bob can have some time alone, but I know better."

My blood freezes in my veins, right to think he suspected something. I glimpse back at him anxiously, before bending over the table to pull a gift placed at the far end over to me. "Stop worrying about Robert. He's been like a father to me for most of my life and doesn't look at me in that way, so no need to be jealous of him if that's what you are."

Nope, Robert isn't the problem here. I am.

Travis inhales deeply. "I'm not worried about anything but you. I've been neglecting you, and I need to handle that before someone else does."

"I doubt if Robert's that someone who will," I mumble, almost sounding irritable.

Yeah, there's no 'almost' about it. I *am* irritable. After collecting the stragglers of gifts to my chest, I turn to leave, nearly running right into Travis. "Why are you crowding me all of a sudden? You can't seriously think something's going on between us."

"Lately, there isn't anything going on between *us* and that's my fault. And you wouldn't be letting another man touch you in any way if there was something going on between us."

"Well, Travis, you picked the wrong day to want to fix what's broken between *us*, annoy the hell out of me with your new stalker tendencies, and hold up Milani from opening her gifts. We'll talk about this when we get home among other things."

He grins. "That damn mouth of yours Trinity, just won't quit, will it? Tonight, I'm going to give you something else to do with it besides talk. Isn't that what you want?"

Not anymore.

Who the hell does he think he is to want to put anything of his near me, even less in my mouth, after the shit he's trying to pull over on everyone?

"Tonight, I'm going to sleep after I get falling-down drunk, and so are you, Travis. Whether you get drunk or not is your business, but I'm advising that you do, so you don't remember when I shoot you down and leave you stuck with blue balls."

He stops smiling. He should. I don't turn Travis down for sex often. He's really damn good at it.

"Are you *that* angry with me for calling off the wedding?"

"You have no idea how angry I am with you, now please move," I demand through gritted teeth, before I sense a big presence coming our way on silent white and tan boat shoes.

Now, Robert's popping up out of thin air with both hands in his pockets, stopping just inside the back doors, and not a moment too soon. "Trinity, do you need help... with the other gifts?"

I don't miss his deliberate pause and got his message. "No, I have the gifts. It's my stalker that I need help with. He won't move out of my way."

Travis smirks then steps closer to me with frost in his blue-gray peepers. "I got your stalker, love," he whispers, "and you haven't seen anything yet."

I decide I don't like his tone or demeanor. He seems cold, ruthless, and threatening—none of the things I've ever witnessed from him before. His head dips, placing his lips are on mine before I can react, but the kiss is just a peck. It feels like a brand to me. Then he steps sideways. If my hands weren't full, I'd wipe his brand away. Considering I'm supposed to be making him think I'm still in love with him, that might be a bad idea, so it's good that my hands are full or I wouldn't give a damn about what is a bad idea.

What I do is walk toward Robert, who's seems to be tunneling into my face with his eyes. I get close enough to notice that he isn't so much as tunneling into my face, but staring at my mouth, like he'd like to wipe Travis' kiss off himself. My stomach starts to tumble around; as if it's happy Robert might be feeling this way, even if it's just coming from his instincts as a father. I pause in front of him, wait for him to let me by. He doesn't. Instead, he reaches out with both hands.

"Give me the gifts. I forgot you hadn't finished eating or your drink when I drafted you into helping me. If you need something else, let me know. I suspect you'll need another drink soon like me… with guests appearing and disappearing and the whatnot."

I trust he's referring to Travis as the whatnot and his sudden interest in reacquiring ground that he's lost in our relationship, and that Robert cares for that about as much as I do. Not at all.

I lock my jaws just to keep from asking Robert why he feels that way and what exactly does he want to do about it. I'm sure I'll agree to whatever. "Maybe P and Rasheed will come back soon," pushes through my teeth, not used to being restrained from saying what's on my mind, even if the words shouldn't be there in the first place.

Robert laughs. "If they do, Rasheed isn't half the man I thought he was."

"What do you know about Rasheed since he became an attorney?"

I need to know whether or not he's any good for Paisley, and if I should run his ass out of town on a rail away from her when we reach Miami tomorrow. Now that I'm paranoid about men with agendas, I'll be investigating more than just my own future dates before I go on them.

Rasheed's a longtime acquaintance of Robert's that used to work for

Bob the Builder as a teen dope trafficker before he decided to go to school to be a criminal lawyer like Rhys. That doesn't mean Rasheed doesn't want something from Paisley. If he does, I'll find out what, and soon.

"Back down, pit bull. Always the mother hen of the three," Robert spews in an amused tone, before scooping the gifts out of my hands by placing his on the backs of mine. "Rasheed's a good man with a rough beginning that I didn't start, but I perpetuated the cycle of black men going to jail or hell when he worked for me and I was glad to send him to school and break at least his downward spiral. Maybe I'll get to send Milani to school if she asks. I won't force her to go though."

I pull my hands back slowly from beneath his, not caring if Travis is standing by. He's surely watching us, and then his footsteps begin rebounding against the floor behind me.

They stop when he stands beside me again. "Maybe you should mention it to Milani when you go outside, Bob… with the gifts, and don't worry about forcing your daughter to do anything. No one can force Milani to do anything she doesn't want to, accept Rhys, and even then I think she capitulates when she wants to."

I catch Travis' repeat performance of the deliberate hesitation before saying 'with the gifts'. He caught the silent messages between Robert and me, and wanted us to know he had. His ears don't miss much. I think it would be very wise to remember that. We need to be more careful about what we say and how we say it around Travis. I seem to need a lot of work on my reactions when both men are around too, so I knit my fingers together in front of my stomach, to stop myself from wringing them nervously while savoring the feel of Robert's touch still flowing like a fluid over the back of them.

"Travis is right, Robert." I say a little too breathlessly, with my stomach doing a lot more than tumbling around. It's doing damn somersaults because of Robert, who probably didn't mean to cause that, but my senses don't care. "You should speak to Milani so she knows she has the option of college. I know she really wanted to go with Paisley and I, but she didn't think her permanent record for being a delinquent in high school would allow her to be accepted into University of Florida. I tried to convince her to go. Although, she can pay for school herself now, thanks to you."

Travis shoves his left hand between mine, unknots my fingers, and pulls our intertwined hands down by our sides. I want to yank away. The angry girlfriend who didn't get married would. The investigative women with one foot out the door of a stagnant relationship that she needs Travis to get comfortable in once again wouldn't.

He looks down at me with a leer on his lips that's not his real smile or reaches his eyes. "Let's go get you fed and drunk, Trinity."

Now, he's monitoring and terminating my conversations with other men.

That's new.

I doubt if it is for him, just for the women who don't really know him. I have a feeling there's more of his hidden qualities waiting to reveal themselves. None of them will be good for me.

Robert's eyes lower to our interlocked fingers then rise again, up to mine that's staring right back at him. "I think we should talk to Milani together, Trinity, in case she decides to tell me where to stick my offer for paying for her college education, and then tries to shove it there herself. No child of mine pays for anything when it comes to their well-being."

That's probably not all we're going to talk about either. I'm sure Robert senses something isn't right with me and Travis, but he can't save me now if he wants me to save him and everyone else that Travis is trying to drag into his scheme later.

Travis exhales. "I think Milani's okay in your relationship now, Bob, and able to talk to you about anything one on one. Plus, she likes to destroy men's *cars* when she's angry."

Robert averts his eyes to Travis. "All the more reason Trinity should be there if Milani goes off. I can leave my daughter in capable hands that'll hold her down while I go hide my car from her."

The vision of that happening is hilarious. "I think you've turned me into your lieutenant while forgetting to pay me, Robert."

"Have I?" His eyebrows draw together.

Travis nods, like someone wanted his opinion. "You have."

The need to circumvent any and all maneuvers he instigates to keep Robert and me apart rises fast within, and I can't resist it. "Just give me a time and place and I'll be there, Robert."

The fingers wrapped around mine begin to tighten like a vise-grip, almost to the point of hurting me. The next hidden quality of Travis' is here already—abusive. I squeeze back and dig my nails that are shaped into the latest design craze, sharp points, into his flesh wherever I can reach until he grunts softly in pain. When his grip slackens, I yank my hand out of his.

Robert's left eye twitches. "We'll need to speak with Milani early, Trinity, before Rhys traps her in her bedroom tonight, and she becomes his willing prisoner. They may not come back out until the baby's birth forces them to. My house at seven o'clock. If she loses it, she'll be well away from her guests and any cars that she'll want to maul."

I laugh like I'm expected to; Milani's new calmer side has been in resident since before she left Miami. I highly doubt if she'll backtrack to her previous aggressive behavior since she was already trying to do and act better before she left, or that Travis is done with the new calculating and aggression in his behavior. I'm more than shook that he just tried a controlling move on me, but he'll soon learn that I'm not a chess piece he can direct around a game board.

"I'll be there with bells on, Robert," I announce, despite the tension rolling off of Travis.

Surely discussing furthering her education with Milani will be talked about at some point, but not for long if it upsets her. I just don't know if I'll be able to discuss Robert's future with Travis' empire without upsetting her too. Or find a way around talking to him about it with her sitting in on the conversation. I'm damn sure not letting her leave Robert's house before I do, or risk making Travis even more suspicious of me and Robert than he already is.

Robert nods suddenly, and then lowers his eyes to the hand that's slightly trembling at my side. His jaw develops a tick before he smiles again and direct his eyes north. "We'll handle this ASAP and quickly… so Travis doesn't miss you from his bed as *his* willing prisoner for long."

"Sounds good, Mr. Elliot," I say just to hit a nerve, like Travis has done to me, and relay a message to Robert; make haste with handling it or I probably won't get old if Travis continues down this path that most women beaters travel.

They get a little more dangerous to their women day by day, until she's helpless and viewed less than human but more than property in his eyes, which makes it easier to kill her. So why in the hell am I thinking about going back home with him? Because I think I can control him too while I'm there, and get out before I'm less than human in his eyes.

Robert smiles at us both before turning around to leave. Travis peers down at me. I stroll away on quivering knees. Robert deposits the last of the gifts on the table. Before Milani can rise from her seat, Rhys is already on his feet and at the back of her chair, tunneling his hands under her elbows and aiding her up. Travis lopes by me in a hurry then takes his seat again. Milani begins to rub together her long graceful fingers that she inherited from her father, on a five foot three stature from her mother that's being swallowed up by baby Jaden and moving toward the gifts.

"Unwrapping time. Whose should I open first?" she asks in a creepy Cruella Deville's voice, just before I throw my first leg over the bench.

It's like she's about to eat a small puppy, and can't decide which one of the 101 Dalmatians is going down first.

I throw my other leg over the bench.

Robert flings his head back on his shoulders. "Shit! I left my gift in the house. Trinity and Rhys please take point beside my child and make sure she doesn't hurt herself. I'm scared she'll regress to the Christmas time when she was about to dive headfirst under the tree. On my bad, she did do that."

Suddenly on duty again, I'm thrilled. Who knows what Travis will do next to me? I sure as hell don't, don't want to be close enough to him to find out. Milani waddles around in a circle until she finds her father, with a blanket of astonishment covering her face.

Robert laughs then kisses her on the forehead. "I was around Milani, even when I wasn't around. Didn't you notice there were always twice as many gifts under the tree every Christmas morning? Jessica didn't have fussed about me spoiling you with you in hearing distance, but she raised pure divine hell when you were out of it. I think she thought it was her job only, but that didn't stop her from mean-mugging me when your back was turned though."

He begins to back away, as more of his presence is revealed in Milani's childhood that she thought was devoid of him. I amble over to the gift table as if I don't have a care in the world, while trying not to break out in a run. It'll be too obvious that I'm trying to put as much distance as possible between me and Travis. He's taken a turn for the worst, and I don't want to investigate his shady business dealings anymore, but I will. Somebody has to.

However, abusive men aren't my type, and I should've seen this behavior coming from Travis a mile away when I first met him, when I should've run. Between his and my wants, the trained psychologist within me was completely psyched out. People that want or already have close ties with narcissists rarely see them for what they truly are until it's too late, which it truly is for me.

His true side has begun to emerge, and he's not going to let go of me now, even after I demand it or pack my bags to leave. He'll follow. Eventually, he'll find me and the war for who really owns my body will begin. I'm trying to avoid that. especially when it's best to keep your enemies close along with a gun. Well, I don't have a gun, so I grab Milani's empty chair, intending to transport it to the side of table she's already standing in front of, tearing into her gifts. I set the chair down as a barrier between me and Travis, while I stand guard with my hands braced on the back rest, well out of Milani's way.

Rhys puts two protective hands on each side of her expanding waistline. "Milani, sit down, love. I'll bring the gifts to you," he issues the edict in the tone of a man that loves his woman and would do anything for her.

She shakes her head. "No sit down yet, baby daddy," she chirps with her hands fingers tunneling under the white bow of a small gift, the mobile for Jaden's crib that's already set up in Milani's bedroom.

My eyes roam to Travis, who's glowering at me, and that's brand new too. Any other time, I'd have found that strange. Since I know who he truly is, it's staggering that I haven't seen that look before now—we butt heads often. Today, he'd clearly set a trap for me. I got away. He really wants to do something about that, but there are too many people around, and most women beaters are cowards that like to stay hidden when they're not in a blind rage or the process of trying to physically destroy the woman that usually wants to give him everything to make him happy. You can't make narcissists happy because you can never give them enough—they're bottomless pits of need-to-possess.

I just need the right somebody to come back so I'll feel safe again. Only Robert seems to know what's going on, if not the dirty details. I don't have to ruin Milani's baby shower by sparking a scene. I will if I must. I like living in one piece and harmony, will pass on being dominated.

Ten minutes drag into the past. I swallow hard, wondering what's taking Robert so long and staring into Travis' eyes, like a frightened deer does headlights. I'm keeping two eyes on his every move now. Dealing with a budding abuser is new to me too, and yes, I'm smart enough to be frightened. At some point, he's going to make the mistake of backing me into a corner when I get away from his control one too many times. Hopefully, I'll have discovered hard evidence of his criminal activity before that happens. If he does back me into a corner before then, I'm coming out of it the best way I know how, and then escaping right then, no matter whose livelihood is at stake.

Milani squeals, still on her feet, when she discovers authentic Gucci apparel in newborn size. "Baby boy's going to be GQ thanks to Paisley. Where is she by the way?" she asks, with a knowing smile on her face.

I guess she approves of Rasheed, and would know just as much about him as Robert does, since he was her attorney while Madeleine's murder case was open. I shrug as an answer to her question, then look away from Travis, while keeping a side eye on him. Robert finally scales the stairs, empty-handed. I release a whoosh of air that I didn't know I was holding.

Starting to see him as my savior when it's supposed to be the other way around, I sneak a desperate peek at Robert. He winks with his left eye. Travis stalks on his right. Who knows what would've happened next if he had caught that? I'm already tired of not knowing what'll happen next in my life.

Robert approaches the closed back doors, places his broad back against the glass, and watches with us. Milani tears through her gifts, slinging the opened one aside to pick up then tear through another one. No one else notices the thick atmosphere that I'm breathing or when Paisley and Rasheed slip quietly up the steps after rounding the corner of the house with huge smiles on their faces.

They're just there suddenly to everyone else, scaring the hell out of David and his date when they retake their seats beside them. I even manage to laugh with my future ex of a problem staring right through me.

"That's everything," Milani announces finally, in front the mess of shredded wrapping paper standing taller than she is on the table.

Robert pushes off the doors, and extracts a set of keys from his pocket, dangling them in the air. "Not everything, love."

An up-to-date Mercedes SUV parked in Robert's driveway, a short walk across their connected lawns away. There should be a red bow on top of the truck now, the reason Robert disappeared. Everyone, except Milani, knows it one of her gifts. She's been eyeing the vehicle all weekend since it mysteriously showed up after our arrival. He lied and told her it belonged to a family that didn't want the sand and sea air to ruin the midnight-black paint job while they used the gated access between the Elliot's rental properties to take their small kids to the beach everyday this weekend.

Milani squeals again, and then snatches the keys *and* her father to her. Travis moves in my side view. I become highly alert, maybe too high, but I'm taking no chances. He's reaching for my abandoned tumbler of Coecoei, tossing the whole drink down his throat. He can do that several times with brown liquid and not even wobble or fall down, so the local firewater isn't going to do much, but the last thing I need is a brooding drunk on my hands. Abusers are even harder to deal with when alcohol is dulling their slim, rational thought process to the wind.

Robert's eyebrow lifts. He cuts his eyes over Milani's shoulder to me, asking silently if I'm in danger. I shake my head, but reserve the right to change my mind later. Suddenly, Milani takes off across the deck as fast as a woman in her eighth month of pregnancy can. Rhys is right behind her, begging her to slow down. She doesn't listen of course. The other guests rise up to catch her reaction when she finds out the vehicle that matches the keys is the same one she's been admiring.

I step around the chair, giving Travis time to get lost in the crowd that's surging down the deck's steps. In front of them is the sidewalk that leads around the house to Milani's driveway. When he lingers, allowing everyone to precede him, my intention to be the last one that joins the crowd works against me. In the middle of the deck, I hesitate, trapped by him who's blocking the steps by simply standing beside them. That's too close for me.

CHAPTER 6

It takes considerable effort to boost my lips up in the corner. "What are you waiting for, Travis? You're going to miss her reaction."

He smiles down at the floorboards, before retraining his gaze on me. "You and I both know the spoiled princess will do the same thing out there that she just did back here, *squeal*! And I'm waiting for you, to apologize for hurting you."

"It's okay. You didn't really hurt me," I murmur, wanting the conversation is over.

He advances. I back up.

He stops in his tracks, shakes his head then wipes a hand down his face. "Fuck! You're lying. Nothing's okay. I went too far in the kitchen and scared you. Now, you're wondering if I'm going to really hurt you. I'm sorry, Trinity. Everything I've done to you in the last two months won't happen again. I swear."

Wow, he shifted to the honeymoon phase of an abusive relationship without even throwing the first punch.

Wasting his time trying to make things right between us before things escalate. They will, but if he keeps this behavior up, I'll have plenty time to unearth his skeletons, finding what I need for an open and shut criminal case against him.

"Don't worry about it, Travis."

Right now, all I want to do is find the others. Even if he doesn't want to see Milani's reaction, I don't want to miss one moment of my girl being happy.

I cross the deck, this time determined to get past him. He stands perfectly still. When I'm a foot away, he steps in between me and the stairs. I have stop again and let him get whatever's on his chest off, but stand my ground. Running backwards will only make him chase. When he says nothing after a few seconds, I sigh wearily. His hands rise. I flinch, prepared to scream the beach down at the first elevated level of pain, and find his testicles with my knee. He cups my face with both hands, moving closer to me instead.

"I never knew how much I really wanted you in my life or what all I'd be willing to do to keep you, Trinity… until now."

I interpret his soft loving words for exactly what they really are, a threat.

"You don't have to do anything to keep me." I'm making no promises that I don't intend to keep.

"For now, I don't, but I'm afraid I let my ambitions get in the way of the best thing that happened to me."

And you're just now figuring that out. Typical!

"Things will get better for us if they're supposed to, Travis."

They won't. I'm not going to let them.

"They have to. I can't let you go."

"When I want you to let go, you'll have no choice, Travis, because I'll already be gone."

"No, you won't, and I won't because I'll fix this. Have to. I truly love you and wish I could go back and change things between us, but I can't because it's the past and I was never supposed to fall in love with you… or anyone else and miss what I had when it's gone."

I take that too for what it is, confirmation that I was a target of his in the bank, even if he tried to add filler for the purpose of subtracting the meaning that he didn't mean to let seep from his mouth, which only makes me angrier with him.

He draws even closer until our fronts are pressed together. "Even as I stand here with my hands on your soft skin, I can feel you slipping away from me, Trinity, like the breeze through my fingers, but I'll make everything up to you. I promise."

Do I want to believe every word that is coming out of his mouth right now? Yes.

Who wants the world, as they know it, to change suddenly? No one, not even a woman in an obvious abusive relationship, surely not the woman that thought she had the perfect man and would never have to worry about if she would be abused. No matter how a woman's world is, it's what she knows, what she's used to, and it's frightening to enter the unknown. Some part of me truly does love Travis, it just isn't the unconditional kind of love that weathers any storm. I want that. Cheating myself out of the chance to have that as long as we're together.

"Stay with me, Trinity. Marry me. Have my babies. Be mine again," he pleads.

Two hours ago, I would've given my left eye and cut off someone else's right leg to hear those words.

His face seems to shrivel up before me suddenly. "Then you really are planning on leaving me?" he asks if he read my thought, but that isn't what happened—I spoke it out loud for him to hear, stupidly.

"I don't think I'll get past how you've treated me, Travis. It went on for far too long and right now, I'm just angry."

"We can get past anything if you want to." He presses his forehead to mine. The skin-to-skin contact should've at least gave me the urge to repair those ties I cut, gave me a mini-thrill, or a few, loose butterflies in my stomach. He seems so sincere in his feelings. I got nothing. My heart is mine, where it has been all along.

"And if I don't want to get past it?" I ask in a monotone.

"Then I'll find some other way to keep you, babe."

This time, I do get something; that cold shiver that's a harbinger of bad things to come. "I feel like that's a warning."

He shakes his head against mine. "It's not. It's a promise, and if I hadn't hurt you in the kitchen two hours..." He steps back suddenly, his hands falling down to his sides, the glower back on his face. "What I did in the kitchen didn't happen two hours ago, Trinity, it was barely thirty *minutes*. What happened to make you give up on us? Was it Robert? Are you cheating on me with him now? Are you in *love* with him?"

I could be in love with Robert, but I was never in love with you, dummy, I think then tilt my head to the side. "You happened to us, Travis, and you don't know when I gave up on us, so don't turn this around on me and Robert. He's the most innocent out of everyone in this shit between us."

"That doesn't answer my question—"

"Trinity, where the hell are you?" Milani's screeching from the front side of her home disrupts him. "We have to ride like we stole this baby before I have to pee because of the other baby!"

Travis shoves his hands in his pockets, props his backside on the wood railing, and crosses his feet while his face returns to a calm state. It's like he was never angry. The psychologist side of me registers the mood swing immediately—another narcissistic trait. The most dangerous and unpredictable of them all.

"Go. We'll discuss this later, but know this. Neither Robert nor anyone else can have you, Trinity. You're mine, and I keep what's mine."

I smile, absolutely sure of what and who I'm dealing with now. "There's the real threat. I was wondering how long it was going to take you to get to it. The Travis I know wouldn't have said something like to me. What happened to you, Travis?" I can't resist asking. It's a 'seeking out the origin of a certain kind of behavior' thing that grips the medical profession tightly and rarely lets us go. "You were the perfect gentlemen two months ago and my everything, but you knew that and ruined it anyway. For what? Another woman? Man? Who pulled you away from me so fast I never saw it coming?"

It's a 'what' that gets the blamed. I just want to know if he'll ever be truly honest with me.

"It was only me and me alone that made the mistake, Trinity. I took your presence in my life for granted. I'll go in depth about what changed me after we get home if you agree to talk to me tonight before you make a decision regarding our future together."

"Alright," I agree quickly.

He can talk. Won't change anything about us. Maybe I'll get a little more insight into his bank business if he decides to tell me the whole truth.

"*Trinity*," Milani screams this time, "I swear I'll drag you around the front of the house by your hair if you don't ride with me and Paisley!"

I should've expected that. The woman can be a beast sometimes when she doesn't get her way.

Travis propels his head in the direction that Milani's voice came from. "Go, Trinity. You know that fool will actually try dragging you away by your hair, and then you two will tear up Aruba fighting," he jokes.

Well, actually he's not joking, but it's still funny, and of course I laugh before moving to the stairs.

He grins. "We'll talk more after you leave Robert's tonight. There are some things you should know about me. Maybe you'll take pity on me and stick around to fix my behavior."

The old cunning Travis is off his leash, with his smooth voice and transparent demeanor unleashed as well, for charming and disarming people. His smile is used like honey to attract bees like me, but he's not attractive anymore. I hurry past him before he changes his mind about talking later. Right now, I need some space and room to breathe properly.

Suddenly, I feel oxygen-deprived now that I had a way or rather permission to leave his company. His eyes bore into my spine until I reach the corner of the house twenty feet away. After turning it, only then do I inhale deeply, filling my starving lungs with clean air packed with sunshine and sea mist, and rush right into a hard chest clothed in… you already know who it is and I do too.

"Jesus, will you stop doing that!" I hiss quietly into the smothering cocoon of Robert's shirt, before looking up into his grim expression.

I back up. He stuffs his phone in his pocket with one hand, reaches down and grabs for my hand with his other one, hauling my further down the side of the house.

"Move before he hears us, Trinity," he orders.

At this point, I should be bristling at being told what to do, but I identify Robert's order as coming from a worried place. I like being bossed around by Travis even less, so I pick the lesser of the two evils this time only.

Robert looks back over his shoulder at me. "You okay?"

"Yeah. You been ear-hustling?" I ask wryly.

He chuckles dryly, quietly. "Yeah, I wanted the son of a bitch to try something else with you, but I guess he's in love now."

He's secretly watching out for me. Lord have mercy!

Check yourself, Trinity.

"Or acting like he's in love. Could be another con job," I suggest lightly, as if anything about this situation shouldn't be taken seriously.

"No, Trinity. I think he finally got what he wanted and he really didn't know how much he cared for you until it was too late and there's a real threat to his relationship with you."

At least I made an impact instead of being just a means to ends for Travis, so I got something out of all if this, a little revenge I didn't know I needed. Nobody wants to be used. However, if Travis really does care for me, that creates a whole other set of problems. God knows I don't need any more of those, especially if there's another threat to Travis that'll make him act even worse towards me.

"What's the threat?" I ask worriedly, certain that Robert doesn't know *he* is the only threat to Travis right now, and Travis still doesn't know that some of his conversation with Blair spilled into my ears.

"Not what, Trinity, but who. Travis isn't an idiot."

"Spell it out for me Robert. *Who's* the threat then? I don't like to assume."

If there's a God in heaven, Robert won't know I have feelings for him or that Travis suspects me of having them. Too many things will have the potential of changing in my world at one time. I'm not prepared to deal with all of it at one time. That takes a lot of strength, and it has been slowly sapped from me as my lack of feelings for Travis twisted me in one way over the last two months. Now, these new feelings for Robert are twisting me in another.

He looks back over his shoulder again. "Me, Trinity, I'm the threat, and he's standing at the corner of the house watching us. Don't look back."

Of course, that's exactly what he'd say, since my luck's gone down the crapper. Looking back is exactly what I want to do as soon as he says not to. It almost hurts to not do it. I can't gauge Travis' mood if I don't, will have to play him by ear after I get back to Miami. I try not to dwell on the fact that Robert knows Travis is leery of him, which is my damn fault, but I'm only assuming about what Robert knows. There's only one way to find out what exactly.

"Why do you think you're the threat, Robert?"

"No time to explain. I'll tell you at the meeting with Milani at seven. For now, keep others close to you. I don't trust Travis around you the same way he doesn't trust me. That's for good reason too. I'll explain that when you get back also. Milani's going to drive around the island until seven. Every ten minutes, she has to pee, so be prepared to make several stops along the way besides dropping David's and Jamal's dates off. As a matter of fact, make a bunch of stops anyway. I need a lot of access to your boy to assess him and make sure he's after what I think he wants and doing what I think he's doing, so I'm going to give him that meeting while all the women are gone. Hopefully, I can set a few traps into place to get him out of your life."

Setting traps means Robert will have to get down into the pit of where he thinks his prey will be next, or kill it himself. I don't want him to do either. Suppose his prey shows up before he sets the trap or catches him off guard. Just the thought of something happening to Robert makes my stomach plummet into my shoes. I begin to develop the first stages of shock; blood flowing through my body too fast and my heart rate skyrocketing.

I don't know how dangerous Travis is. Neither does Robert, who seems like he has an idea though, since he's trying to get all of the women out of the house. That doesn't make me feel any better about Robert's safety. His concern is still dragging me closer to him in all the ways that could destroy my relationship with the Elliot's as I know it.

Before I can order him to not set any traps for me, we're already turning the next corner of the house and walking into David's, Jamal's, Rhys', and Rasheed's space that they're taking up on Milani's front lawn. They're group together, wearing not the nicest of looks on their faces while they talk amongst themselves. I don't know how much they already know about Travis, nor do I want them to get hurt for knowing too much. Silently, I pray their safety is in God's plan, and take comfort in the fact that Robert won't be completely alone with Travis.

When we skirt around the men, I murmur, "Robert, I don't want you to meet with Travis. Or wait until I've told Milani know what the hell is going on."

He squeezes my hand gently. His touch is reassuring and sending tiny bolts of lightning up my wrists. I'm certain this is the second time I've experienced that, both times today with Robert, and that I'm flying high, which is quickly becoming addicting. I want to experience it again, even if he has no idea what he's doing to me.

We reach the passenger side of Milani's truck trimmed in chrome, as well as sitting on it. The rims make the vehicle look even more expensive, right up Milani's alley. She'd rather ride in style or walk. Robert opens the passenger's door with his free hand, then lifts his arm attached to the hand that I'm still gripping as if it'll mean life or death for me if I let go. Oddly, I think it will in some way, and I haven't even kissed the man. I crouch under his raised arm while looking up at him pleadingly, then stand before him with my back to the women in the truck.

"Don't do this, Robert," I whisper.

He smiles, and it's brighter than the sun and warms me up just a little. "I'll be fine and so will you, love. Milani's driving isn't that bad."

She smirks from the driver's seat. "Oh my father has jokes today."

"That's every day, Milani," Paisley comments, while I have to let his hand go to climb into the seat unwillingly. Only God knows how much I don't want to leave him, and I really hope it's *only* God that knows.

Robert grips my shoulder more firmly, while closing the door. Suddenly, I feel abandoned while I sit with the two girls that have had my back for almost a lifetime. Now, I need a drink desperately. Robert's changing everything about me without even knowing it. How in the hell am I going to hide my feelings from my girls if I can't even hide them from myself?

David's and Jamal's date sit in the back with Paisley, whose sitting bitch, her favorite spot for a few reasons. She can stick her head between the seats and literally be in the middle of the conversation when it gets good, but not have to deal with Milani's amateur NASCAR driving up close and personal. Paisley also likes to stretch out and sleep on road trips or talk quietly on her phone without interruptions and feeling cramped while Milani and I fuss about her speeding. It never occurs to me to get in the back and let Paisley stomp on the imaginary passenger side brakes when Milani's riding up on the back end of another car too fast, but I've always confronted problems head on.

Since she's been pregnant, maybe Milani's no longer into speed racing with herself and other cars that don't know they're in a race, which will give me time to find a way to explain what's going on with her father and me without Milani biting my head off. If Robert's meeting with Travis is giving me minor heart palpitations, I can't imagine what it'll do to her. She doesn't deserve to be left in the dark when danger could be so close to everyone she loves. How do I explain what he means by setting a trap for Travis when I don't even know what that means yet? And how do I even kick this conversation off in the first place?

This isn't the type of everyday conversation you have with your best friend, especially when her father's involved and it's your entire fault. All I know right now is that seven o'clock won't get here fast enough, so I can push some of the explaining off on Robert. According to Milani's dashboard clock surrounded by woodgrain, I have two hours to locate a solution to a problem I can't seem to face for the first time, head on or otherwise.

Milani cuts her eyes at me too many times to count while dropping the guys' dates off on opposite ends of the island. First, we make a pit stop on Baby Beach for the beauty that looks a lot like me, and then drive towards the other side of the island to Arashi Beach, where Jamal's latest submissive may live. That poor chick doesn't know what she's going to be getting herself into if she sleeps with him.

Speaking of poor chicks, a round trip around Aruba from one end to the other is only 20 miles, the whole island six miles wide, and there's only so much time I can spend chewing on my acrylic nails. Poisoning myself which is way better than facing Milani, and staring anxiously out the window. Both of my girls are going to notice that something's wrong. I'm not complaining about Milani's driving. She still speeds by the way. Isn't driving fast enough for me today.

"Trinity," Milani calls, as soon as Jamal's girl shuts the back door.

I watch her cross the lush green grass in front of her small house with a thatched roof. "Yeah, love."

"You're literally fretting over there. I didn't know you were capable of that. What the hell's up with you? I've speeded all the way to Nina's house just to get a reaction from you, and you said nada."

"Okay."

I turn back to the window and start chewing on my nails again. Robert is stuck with doing *all* of the explaining at this point. I wish we were back at the house already. Rather face Travis than Milani right now, and need to know for myself that Robert's okay. For that, I need a valid excuse to get us there, which I come up with in a whole hour.

"What the hell are you worried about, Trinity?"

"Your father's going to explain it to you when we get back, and we need to go back... because I haven't taken my birth control for today."

I forgot to take it on time at two o'clock, but that's Robert's and Travis' fault.

"From what you told me, you and Travis aren't doing the do anyway, so screw your pill. Hmmm... that didn't sound right did it?"

Paisley and I both laugh despite my turbulent emotions.

"No, Milani. It didn't, so don't say ever that again."

Milani sobers. "But seriously, Trinity, your girls are here with you and you don't seem all that into Travis anymore. We noticed you spazzing out on him when he touched you under the table. I saw my father holding your hand like you were his little girl and damn near dragging you to the away from Travis. Having to drag you away isn't out of the ordinary since it's almost impossible to get you away from Travis on the weekend. It did look suspicious when you didn't seem like you wanted to let my father's hand go though. You know my father won't hurt Travis for hurting you until he can cover it up and keep his ass in the clear, so for now you know your boy's safe. You also only know David, Rasheed, Rhys, and Jamal in passing and from what I've told you about them, so you have to be worried about my father, and he said not to come back before seven and to take you straight to his house, not mine. Why?"

Since Milani's doubtful of me now, it's time to come clean with her. I start trying to collect my words and thoughts.

"Damn it, T!" she yells then frowns. "Something has got you shook and you're damn near unshakeable. What is it? Is it my father? If it is, fine, but he wouldn't tell me anything on the phone because he didn't have time, but you do, so tell me now! Or I'll go straight to Travis and make a scene when we get back, Trinity."

I breathe in deeply. "Threat not necessary, Milani. I know you will, and I was going to tell you what's going on anyway." When I found the right way to say it.

She smiles widely. "Good girl."

"You're such a brat, Milani," I snipe lovingly.

"True," Paisley chirps in without hesitation, which is odd for her.

She doesn't have a mean bone or cruel way about her, but she'll tell you the truth, when she finds the courage. I see no cups of liquor in the backseat, so Rasheed must be rubbing off on her in only two days' time. Maybe, he's what she's needed in her life all this time, or she's finally growing up.

Milani bangs her hands on the wheel.

Paisley slaps her across the shoulder gently. "Will you chill, Milani? Damn! Good stories take time to get out."

Milani glares back at her before turning her eyes back to the road. "P, you don't understand. Daddy wanted Milani away from Travis so badly he had me hollering my head off on demand to get her around the house. Something's going on with these two. They're both acting funny. He hasn't let me out of his eyesight for eight months. Suddenly, he's telling me to drive for two hours and where to deliver her when we get back, like she's a package he's been waiting for and determined nothing will happen to it until it gets to him. He's been treating no one else like that but me."

It would be so easy to lie to her right now just to save myself from this conversation, but we don't lie to one another, and they don't try to save themselves from conversations they don't want to have with me… not that often.

"And if I say it's something besides family drama, Milani?" I ask, testing the waters.

"I'll believe that too."

"And you're fine with it?"

"I have to be, if it's the case of lust that I think it is. You're both adults, and what you do together has nothing to do with me as long as you don't hurt one another, but I expect you two to act like adults if this thing doesn't last between you."

"Hold on, Sister Kate. I didn't say we had a thing, and Robert sees me as a—"

"Don't say daughter," Paisley interrupts.

I look back over my shoulder apprehensively. "Why not, P?" What do they know that I don't?

"Because I don't have permission to call him anything other than Mr. Elliot like you do," she mentions with an impish grin, dumbfounding me with that revelation.

It didn't occur to me that Robert only extended the privilege of using his first name to only me. Yep, these girls know too much, and why do I feel special because I'm the only one that has privileges with Robert?

This doesn't mean anything until he explains why Paisley doesn't have the privilege, so get over yourself now, Trinity.

Getting over myself now.

"Fine," Milani snaps, "Maybe there are two of us that can call him daddy. Big deal! Now, spill Trinity, because calling my father by something other than Mr. Elliot and how I feel about it isn't all that's weighing on your mind. You're still fretting with your eyes. What has Travis done that involves my father?"

How in the hell does Milani know already?

CHAPTER 7

"Jesus, you really should've been a damn detective, Milani," I spew before turning sideways in my seat to face both girls.

No point in avoiding the conversation now.

Milani grins. "Apparently, mothers gain super hearing so they can hear their babies cry which means I heard you whispering to my father. Now spill."

It takes me about thirty minutes to go through every sordid detail of Travis' undercover operation that I know of with one 'pit stop for the bathroom' interruption and without mentioning the touch that put her father on my radar. Both women's eyes widen until they're about to pop right out of their heads, as I clarify what I heard during Travis' phone call. For another thirty minutes, I have to convince Milani not to turn around to protect Robert

By now, I've managed to assemble my thoughts, find some of my composure, and remember that Travis isn't meeting with Robert. "Right now, your father's being Bob the Builder, Milani. No ass covering from outside sources needed at this point, or I'll kill Travis' lily white ass and his goons with questionable race my damn self if anything happens to him."

"If Travis hurts my father, I'll kill him first. I never liked that dude."

"I know, Milani. I just wished you had found a way to tell me what is it specifically that you don't like. I could've cut Travis off at the pass... or at the bank before now."

Her face scrunches up at me, like she's thinking deeply, or has to use the bathroom again. "You were happy, T, would've cut me off first without meaning to, and I needed you. It's nothing specific about Travis that I don't like. It's everything, and just a feeling I have about him. He's dark through and through, although he's as white as Casper. I can recognize the darkness in him because I use to seek out people like him, like Tariq. They're hard to love even for a little while because they're constantly shifting your world around, preparing it for when they flip on you and you can't get away. But I knew better than to let Travis come in between us by getting on your bad side if I stated my honest opinion of him. Sometimes, honesty isn't the best course to take, and I was already on your bad side with my own mess, so no thank you very much to the outside help. I just waited until he flipped on you like he's doing now and *made* you cut him off."

Then she jerks her head toward me. "You *are* done with him right? Because I just gave you my honest opinion of him and you two aren't exactly broken up yet."

"I'm gone in the mind, Milani. It's the physical ties like the life I built with him and whatever he's tied up with that's keeping me in his orbit for the time being. I need time to find someplace else to live then break away while investigating his ass. He can keep the house. His father brought it, but Travis won't need it after he goes down, and he needs to go down if he had anything to do with Madeleine's murder. I can't believe he's using people's troubles to make a profit when he'll inherit five banks. And last but not least, he duped me into thinking he was a perfect fit to be my everything when I wasn't his. I probably missed out on the man meant for me while fooling around with Travis' trifling ass." Or maybe I didn't, but only time will tell.

Milani nods. "Travis didn't have anything to do with Madeleine's death though. It truly is coincidence and bad luck for his boys who were circling her pharmacy while Kenu was circling Madeleine's house, but Travis is still not a good man. He puts up a good front. Deep down inside, he's rotten to the core, probably feels entitled to people and their possessions like Tariq did, and probably not capable of love. Most people with Travis' and Tariq's energy aren't."

"A psychopath is what Travis is," I murmur, "and it would be a miracle if he really loves me."

She nods while going into a curve on an almost empty road with very small lanes. "I bet he loves you though."

I do a double-take twice, almost dislodging my ponytail. "Why in the hell do you think that?"

She grins. "You're beautiful and smart. Karma's a bitch, and coincidence sets your ass up by performing miracles like making the unlovable and those unable to love *fall* in love, putting people in prime positions just so Karma can fuck with them big time." Milani would know.

"That's why Karma and Coincidence are sisters," Paisley pipes up, after listening intently for almost an hour straight.

Milani and I chant, "Great minds," before laughing about coming to the same conclusion as Paisley

She shakes her head solemnly between the seats. "Poor Travis. If coincidence set up the meeting at the bank just so he can meet and fall in love with the woman that'll get him what he wants the most then take his ass down with it, he's in for a world of hurt."

"Don't dish it if you can't take it," Milani adds while circling around Eagle Beach.

The rest of the ride's quiet, while we try to enjoy the scenery and each other's company, but my thoughts center on Robert. I'm sure Milani's are too, every second we're joyriding. However, Paisley's taking her first nap, staking her claim on the new backseat, and nobody will ever be able to sit back there with her again without her letting them know in silent but obvious ways that their company isn't wanted. We have ten minutes to go before seven o'clock arrives. I begin to get a little jumpy, but Milani hasn't received a call or text saying 'come back' or 'your father's hurt' yet. I take that as a good sign, but I need proof that Robert's okay, like touching his body for myself.

"So, Trinity, when are you going to tell me about your feelings for my father?" Milani asks out of the blue.

I panic. Paralysis sets up shop in my body. I thought I had avoided this conversation, and confident that nothing will ever come of my feelings for her father anyway. Well, besides bringing a whole lot of uncomfortable moments to me when around him until I find the man for me. There's no point in talking about it if you ask me. Unfortunately for me, somebody did ask.

"Ah, Milani—"

"Don't start lying to and changing up on me now. You tell it like it is about everything else. I'm not mad with you if you want to bang my father, if that's what's got you worried. He deserves a good woman that won't hurt him intentionally and try to use him for his money."

"I wouldn't do—"

"I know that," she interrupts again. "And that's why I'm not mad with you. I used to worry about what woman would get her hands on my father's change, but with you I know he'll be in good hands. If anything happens between you two, it'll be real lust or love. Neither of you do anything halfway. My father's getting older and has no time for games. He needs a woman that knows her own mind and can take him as he is. He hasn't found the real love of his life yet, and he's not going to change for anyone. So whatever quirks he has, the woman in his life is stuck with them. You can handle them because you'll let him know where to get off at and walk away without hard feelings. So enjoy my father's body while you can."

"Are you through cutting me off rudely?"

She snickers and nods.

"He doesn't see me like that, Milani."

Paisley sighs from the backseat where she's laying on her back with one hand below her head. I whip my eyes around to her who's already staring at me.

"For the love of God, Trinity, the man called you his love before you got in the truck and I don't even think he or you realized it yet. He only calls Milani that. Travis' bullshit has got your mind so twisted you're not even yourself right now and missing things that you should be catching, like he's trying to start an empire with prescription pills. That was Madeleine's business and why Travis' goons were circling her pharmacy. Mr. Elliot already knows this. You would too if you weren't watching Travis too closely to see what's right in front of you. He's hoping that Mr. Elliot can put him in contact with suppliers or someone that can. What else can Mr. Elliot do for anyone concerning the game since he's out of it now?"

Then her hand rises up and slaps the seat below her hips. "Bang Milani's fine ass father already so you aren't distracted by wanting to when Travis starts trying to twist up the little world that you two created together until you can't find your way out of it or away from him. Mr. Elliot's trying to prevent all of that by getting into Travis' head first, then him out of your life and save you at the same time."

I huff air. Paisley just hit the mother lode with her assessment of my situation. She should've been a psychologist or detective herself instead of a paralegal. A career that needs higher education and gives Paisley breeding in her parents' opinion, but it's not high profile enough to make her superior to any man they want her to marry. However, she didn't hit on why I feel like I'm dying inside, and I need her assessment on that too, just like I needed that hope that Milani was giving me before this shit storm began. I should've turned to my girls before it kicked off, another mistake I plan to rectify.

"Okay, so you've solved the puzzle, Inspector Booker. Now, I need hard evidence… but that has nothing to do with Robert getting into Travis' head to get him out of my life and scaring the hell of out me with his way of doing it, Paisley, which is why I'm… fretting as Milani claims." Suppose I lose him before I get the chance to tell him how I feel? I can deal with rejection; it's the unknown that frightens me.

Paisley sits up and thrusts her head between the seats. "That's your problem, Trinity, trying to do things the right way all the time while trying to avoid making mistakes. Sometimes, the magic's in the mistake. Travis was one that you thoroughly enjoyed, but even he wasn't a mistake for you. You chose him carefully just like he did you, and you haven't cried over anything he's done to you in the past few months, like most women do when we they think they're losing everything they love. If he had your heart, you would've cried even if you weren't a complete control freak, but he never had it. It was never meant for him. You know it, and didn't want him to have it anyway because you need control over your emotions every minute of the day. And that's because you've already learned at thirteen that you can't control what happens *to* you, but you're still a control freak, so the next best thing to have unlimited control over is how you react and behave, oh and over your heart. There are only a few things and people that you invest it in, like family, your job, and the image that Travis presented to you."

She begins to wave her left hand about. "Yeah, he's all put together on the outside, which works for you since you hate messiness with a capital H, but you went too far with the 'avoiding involving your heart' thing because dude isn't safe in the least. He's disturbing, even with his clean cut appearance. If Milani and I saw through it to the darkness in him from the minute we met him, *you* didn't see that about him because *you* didn't want to."

My mouth drops while I try to absorb that Paisley, of all the shy people in the world, just gave it to me raw and uncut, until I begin to laugh and can't stop. "Baby Paisley's giving me advice and telling me off in the same sentences, Milani. I thought that was my job."

Milani snorts beside me. "P doesn't seem so much like the baby of the clique anymore now, does she?"

"Hell no," I chirp between giggles.

Paisley sits up in the backseat. "And I'm not through yet. If you're this worried about Mr. Elliot, Trinity, I'm sorry to tell you honey, but he's already touched your heart, and right now you probably have no clue how he feels about you. You of all people should've figured that out too by now since that's your job, but you can't see straight because of Travis, and that's the way he wanted you to be until things started to fall into place for him. Then it was 'all bets are off', like the wedding. Lust and love likes to blind you too. They can't work on you if you can see what they're doing to you, and you're scared shitless that you'll never find out how Mr. Elliot really feels about you if Travis hurts him. He won't, but Travis is about to get a taste of what love can do to your heart, and trust me when I say Mr. Elliot will rock your world. Even if it's just for one night, you'll have a beautiful mistake to remember. The man looks like he could bang—"

"Paisley!" I yell before she finishes.

It's actually more terrifying to know what she's about to say than it is to *not* know.

She giggles. "Hey, I've been around you two for most of my life. You two have been through the gambit of situations. I've learned a few things, like how to bang sugar out of a cake from Milani, judge people then get them on the right track from you. Now can we go back to the house, Milani? I actually love Mr. Elliot like a father and don't want anything to happen to him either. Trinity's going to have a heart attack if we don't go back soon and check on him, even if she's not saying it outright. Rasheed needs to learn about my banging skills before I go home and all hell breaks loose."

"Sugar out of a cake, Paisley!" I howl, amused. "*That* sure as hell doesn't sound right. Don't say that to me again either."

Milani laughs softly, shaking her head. "It's almost time to go back anyway... right after I make a pit stop."

We stop by a public restroom at a nearby gas station on Eagle Beach before finishing the five minute drive to Robert's house. The atmosphere in the car is quiet as the dead and tense, laughter long gone. Neither of us knows what we're going to find when we get to his house. Milani turns onto a single lane then drives slowly down it until she reaches the fork between hers and Robert's double-driveways and identical houses. They're positions at an angle, giving them each a view of the other's front door.

Everyone seems to sit up a little straighter in their seat, turning their heads to make sure there are no surprises waiting for us under the huge trees that surround both properties and throw massive amounts of shade.

Somehow, it seems even darker below the enormous leaves, around their broad trunks. None of the guys who were standing outside when we left are anywhere to be found, which only serves to ramp up my apprehension. They should've been watching Robert's back.

My nerves and muscles strum tight with rising tension. I grab the sliver of aluminum for a door handle, almost jump out of the car while it's still moving, to go find Robert for myself. I'm no stunt woman.

"Jesus, Milani! Park the damn car already."

"Jesus, Trinity," she mimics. "Calm the fuck down. Everyone's okay, and you never jump head first into anything. That's how I got shot, remember?"

If Rhys hadn't been there, she would be dead too.

"You don't know if everyone's okay. No one's anywhere to be seen. Just stop the damn car and let me out *then* park."

"You're crazy if you think I'm letting you get out alone. Daddy is fine and so are you. No one's stupid enough to try anything with all of us around."

"You don't know if everyone's still around, Milani. We're still in the damn *car*!"

Three seconds too long later, she parks beside Robert's red Camaro that he gave to her in Miami. She gave it back because her plans to get the hell out of Miami after she found Madeleine's murderer didn't require a vehicle. Milani wanted a plane as transportation.

I pull the lever for the door and push my weight against it at the same time. So damn anxious, even waiting for the microsecond that it takes for the door to open after my push only serves to make me angry. Nothing ever works exactly how or when you need it to. I think I should already be on the outside of the truck by now.

When my feet hit the paved strip of driveway between the cars, the ten steps it takes me to get to Robert's white front door then turn the brass knob without knocking first takes too long too. With my heart beating in my ears, I push the door open, and find Robert standing alone in the middle of his tan floral couches plastered with palm tree leaves and facing each other in the living room, with his phone up to his ear and back to me.

Janine's *Hold Me* plays softly in the background. The haunting sounds of that song only serve to make me even more worried about the sight of him being alive and well. I truly need the man to hold me. Just only touching him would've work two hours ago. The amount of need swirling through me is colossal, enough to send me into paranoia in the time it takes for me to walk around the first couch facing away from the front door, right up to his backside. Milani took too long letting me out of the car and I'm about to go off on somebody, like the man that I want to hold me. Yep, my heart's definitely involved in this situation.

"They're here. I'll call you back, Jamal and Seth." Robert ends the call with a swipe of his finger.

"Don't ever send me off again," ejects out of my mouth.

He swivels around with a frown on his face, still holding the phone in the air. "Excuse me."

Milani continues pass us toward the kitchen entrance in the top left corner of the room. "Oh shit, Paisley. The aggressive Trinity's in resident. Let's go to the kitchen and find something to eat while they work this out... or work out each other."

Paisley's lips poke out. "But I can't learn anything from them if I don't listen in," she whines, while following Milani out of the room. "She didn't even ask where Travis is."

Milani stops in her track, then reverses to the end of the walkway near me and Robert. She slings her arm over Paisley's shoulder. "Of course she didn't ask, Ms. Bang Sugar Out Of A Cake. Trinity no longer gives a shit about him, and you know enough as it is, with your nosy ass."

Paisley's dark head filled with tight spirals that reach the middle of her back tilts upwards. "I'm not nosy, sis. I just like to be informed of what's going on around me with the people I love."

"That's the definition of nosy, P." Milani's voice drifts away, along with the conversation between them, into the kitchen until there's no noise but my heavy breathing boomeranging in my ears.

My chest heaves, as if I've completed a marathon. Robert's forehead is creased with millions of wrinkles, his eyes bright with confusion. He doesn't know he's in a standoff, but he's about to find out.

"What happened while we were gone?"

He steps to me. Scent of man, Aspen cologne, and cooked food waft around me, creating an illusion of home, and a predator. I would love to be his prey, and yeah, I find that abnormal too, since I've never wanted to be caught by anyone before this moment.

"Why did you say don't ever send you off again?"

"Don't answer a question with a question. Your daughter took too long letting me out of her truck so I could check on you… and I asked first."

He thrusts his hands in his pockets. "What happened is exactly what was supposed to, Trinity. I gave Travis a meeting. He gave me his pitch. I told him I'd think about helping him out and let him know by the end of the week my decision. He went to Milani's house where he sleeps. It was business as usual for Bob the Builder." Whatever that means.

"Are you going to help him?"

He sneers at me. "Oh, I'm going to help him alright."

His grin is the most vicious that I've ever seen on anyone's face. I've talked with people from all walks of life with different levels of maliciousness creeping around them like vines, and tried to help them do better. Robert's presence, malicious or not, is just comforting to me. I don't want him to risk doing anything that can take him away from Milani, even if he doesn't want me like I do him. She and Jaden need him more than I do.

"What are you going to do?"

"That's for me to know, Trinity. The less you know about what I'm doing, the better, but there are a few things you should know." His explanation makes me seethe. I need to know everything and be able to reduce it down to its simplest form in a matter of minutes.

"Better for whom, Robert? I've probably had three to four new health conditions develop since you decided to meet with Travis. Who knows which is going to kill me before you're out of the middle of this mess?"

His lips twitch, the maliciousness of the smile on them lessening in intensity. "When did you decide you wanted me, Trinity?"

"When what? Ah… shit…" I stammer to a complete stop, feeling like I'm on a hot seat.

Apparently, Robert faces things head on too. I shouldn't answer his question, not when I know the answer could still change so many lives. Not knowing exactly how it will is why I hesitate, but his eyes seem to be already searching for the answer in mine. I swear he'll find it soon, which doesn't mean he'll do a damn thing about my feelings for him. I'm not a coward either. His rejection just might be what I need to get my head on straight concerning him.

I prop both fists on my hips first. "When you touched me in Milani's kitchen. If you had never done that, I'd still be willingly oblivious to your scent, and what your hand feels like on my body… and what makes you more man than most."

His smile deepens; the intent back in it, if not a little more. Somehow, I know it's not the same grin he had while discussing Travis. Robert looks like he's ready to eat someone alive.

"What makes me more man than most?" he asks suddenly.

I can't help but smile back. "Fishing for compliments, Robert?"

"What if I am?"

"Then I'll give them to you. Your inner strength, you have it in spades and it pours off of you and fucks with my mind big time. I never noticed it in all the years that I knew you." Doesn't mean I didn't know it was there though, just that he was off limits to me, so I ignored it.

There's nothing I wouldn't give to still be able to ignore it *and* keep my heart to myself again. Losing everyone I love scares the hell out of me.

"And then I touched you?" he asks in a rhetorical tone.

I take a deep breath, preparing for whatever happens next as best I can. "Yes, and then you touched me."

"What if I touch you again?"

"I'm sure I'll have the same reactions that I've been experiencing all day. Why?"

"Because… I want to touch you again just to make you explain what you're feeling and where, in great detail. Didn't want to stop touching you after the first time. Couldn't you tell?"

It takes a moment for me to absorb his words, and cherish them. "Honestly Robert, no I couldn't tell. I thought you were just comfortable with being around me like you've always been for seventeen years… and Paisley's convinced Travis has screwed up my observation skills."

"In that case, I *was* comfortable around you, Trinity."

He was *comfortable. Past tense. Shit, I knew I'd screwed everything up with letting Robert get to me.*

I don't know how to undo it. The steady beating in my chest loses its tempo again, before it resumes its normal rhythm. I've screwed everything up now, and might as well finish the job by finding out what happens next and a way to deal with it later. "And now?"

"I want to be in you, on you, next to you, under you—"

I hold my palm up between us, cutting him off before the steady beating in my chest speeds up anymore and my lungs forget how to function completely. "No more, Robert. I have my limits."

He harrumphs softly. "Have I breached them yet?"

"That was this morning. Now, I'm just trying to stay sane around you."

"Can't have that, now can we?"

He bows his head. Mine tilts back so I can look directly in his eyes. His hands dive through the space between my elbows and waist just before they both take up resident against my spine. My poorly functioning heart goes completely on the fritz. His eyes drift downward, to my mouth. My head begins to lighten in weight until it feels like its floating above my body, but my senses tune into his energy like a missile seeking heat. He's driving me out of my right mind.

"Whatever it is that you're going to do to me Robert, do it now before I'm lying on the floor."

He molds his front to mine, trapping my harden nipples between us.

That's actually painful when you want someone this much, and I never knew that until now. Well, at least his mouth's exactly where I've wanted it to be all day, finally.

CHAPTER 8

Soft pillows with an electrical charge are what his lips feel like on mine. These pillows want something from me. It feels like everything as they press into mine. My lips press back before opening beneath his, ready to give him whatever he wants in any amount. His tongue slowly slips inside my mouth and begins to stroke, suck, and sip from mine, driving me bat shit crazy in an instant. I close my eyes and let my head recline between my shoulder blades. It's too heavy to hold up under the sudden pressure of desire spiking and weighing down on my body like a ton of bricks.

A steady throb begins at the apex of my thighs, as if that section of my body is jealous that his tongue's flicking in and out of my mouth, not working on the mouth in the southern region of my body. I knew he would make me want to beg him to kiss me everywhere. I *would* beg if his tongue wasn't doing a slow twirl around the tip of mine, impeding speech. Then his head slowly rises above mine, halting the kiss before I'm ready for it to end. I stand with a tight grip on his upper arms while my chest yanks air in it. Not sure when I dared to touch him like a woman would a man she wants. Not sure if I can let him go at this point either.

What kind of man can make a woman's body hate parts of itself because he didn't pay one section as much as attention as he did the other?

The kind of man that can make you cry, Trinity, if he ever walks away, and someone might as well stick a fork in your heart because it's done for.

So done for, his minty breath coming in soft gasps and fanning over my face feels like his essence is soaking into mine and altering my DNA. Sweet Jesus, I'll never be the same.

He swallows hard while his eyes dig into mine like onyx shovels. "Trinity, we have to stop, sweetheart, or I'll take you right here with my daughter and your adopted sister in the next room, and we'll won't get to talk until much, much later."

I won't lie and say I wouldn't be all in if he wanted to lay me down right here. Currents of anticipation shoot through my abdomen. It wouldn't take Milani and Paisley long to figure out that something scandalous is happening in this room, and run screaming out the back doors, giving us some much needed privacy. Or at least Milani would skedaddle. Paisley, I'm not so sure about.

A rock hard bulge is pressing into my abdomen above trembling thighs, which I had no idea were doing that until now. Since Robert's suffering just as much as I am, I decide to let him walk away, for now. I need to catch my breath and find out what all is he's willing to tell me at this point, while relocating one thong sandal-clad foot behind me, intending to step back. Robert's arms tighten around me. His fingers press into my spine, and drag me toe to toe with him again.

"Not yet, sweetheart," he whispers hoarsely.

The mini-thrill that I expected to get from Travis on the deck triples blazes a path from the top of my head to the bottom of my feet, leaving me light-headed. All I'm sure of at this point is that I'm in the arms I should've been in from the time I ran into Robert at the coffee shop. I don't think I'll be ready to ever step back from him again. That's frightening, but a good frightening. The kind that makes me want to open doors with my heart that I never wanted to with any other man.

"I'll stay," I murmur, with a stupid smile playing on my lips.

He frowns. "Sweetheart, that's what I have to tell you. You can't stay. You have to go home with Travis and pretend nothing has changed until I can catch him in the act of doing something illegal that'll put his ass away for life, longer if I have my way."

As in go home to Travis, right now?

The thrill racing through me is replaced with a chill immediately, a spine-numbing cold one. I no longer want to go anywhere with Travis, even less leave Robert here.

"What are you saying? That I need to still be his girlfriend?"

Before now, I was prepared to do that. Not anymore. Feels like a death sentence coming from Robert's mouth. I belong with him now.

He nods, stroking my spine. "And all that being his girlfriend entails if you want him to continue on with business as usual."

My fingers dig into his arms. "Shit, Robert. I would've happily done that before now, and planned to. I thought that was my only choice, but this… everything has changed. I don't want to leave you before I figure out where we go from here."

"We'll have plenty of time to figure it out together, love." He rocks me gently. "And I know everything's changed between us." Then his smile fades away, as if it was never there. I'm not going to like his next words. "But we can't be together if we want to catch his ass up."

One touch and a kiss, that's all I get from the man that has taken the very essence of me and adjusted it so that it's only compatible to him. I can barely believe that was all it took, and now he's telling me that I have to live twisted up like this with another man. There's nothing I can do about it if Robert doesn't want me to do anything.

Since I don't ever overstep someone else's bounds who don't want me to, I release one of his arms, and swipe the back of my hand across my mouth. If I was going to be able to be anywhere near Travis and act normal, I'm going to have to forget everything about Robert's touch. In other words, I'll be doing a whole lot of praying and drinking until Travis is gone from my life for good. Nothing about Robert is forgettable.

His hand flashes before my face and then my hand is behind his back. "Don't do that, Trinity," he growls. "Never wipe me off of you."

What the hell is he? A ninja?

"Jesus Christ, Robert! Give me some warning next time!" I hiss, angrier than I've ever been. He's pulling me in two different directions. "What else am I supposed to do if I have to go home with Travis? Do you know what your mouth just did to me? I can't have your touch on me and be with him too. "

He grimaces. "Whatever you felt, Trinity, I did too. But if we want him out of your life, we're going to have to play his game his way while I work behind the scenes to take him out of the game period. Do you think I *want* to tell you that this is the way it has to be? That hard evidence's the only way to get rid of him without killing him?"

"At this moment, I prefer to kill him," I snarl, before my words register with my right mind, pushing my eyes out of my head. I'm not a killer, have only ever contemplated murdering my brother's killer who was never found, but to want to do that for Robert and not even hesitate to say I would is another thing. How deep does my feeling go for this man? "Shit, Robert, I didn't mean to say that."

He huffs. "Yes, you did, and I would too for you, if I didn't think you would look at me differently. You would, and I'm not risking losing you before I've even claimed you as mine. For now, we do things Travis way, but only if you want to. If you stay here with me, he's not going anywhere, and the only thing he'll do incriminating is whatever it takes to get you back. The law will let him get away with committing domestic crimes too many times to count before they lock him up, and then I *will* kill him. Do you understand that?"

I nod, stupid glad that he's at least willing to kill for me too. "Have you ever killed someone?" Yeah, it's an unintelligent question to ask at this point since everyone knows that Bob the Builder's a criminal, but I never liked or depended on secondhand information.

Robert's grin dissipates. The atmosphere gets thick like it does when I'm dealing with a client who has a horrific story to tell and doesn't want to. I wait patiently for him to tell me the truth, with my bottom lip tucked between my teeth, anxiety buzzing through me like a nest of bees. Yet, nothing will change a thing about how I feel for him.

He glances over his shoulder before his eyes find mine again. "I've done what I had to do to keep my image, and that's all you need to know for now. One day, I'll tell you all my secrets. I don't know who's listening right now, and no one's supposed to ever know what I've done in my life. I can't risk anyone knowing what I do and saying or doing something that gives Travis any reason to believe I'm not on the up and up. What I do need to tell you about right now needs to be said in front of the others so I say it only one time. I need to call the guys in here. Meet me in the kitchen."

Robert sounds like he's some kind of government agent or undercover cop. What kind of criminal talks like that? I'm slightly comforted by the fact that Robert won't be risking jail time himself to get Travis out of my life, but I truly don't care what happens to Travis after this either. Would rather go with Robert wherever he's going.

However, clinging to him will only give me more memories that'll haunt me when I leave Aruba. Once again, I need distance from Robert that I really don't want, starting to hate that I do need it. Requesting more information about him won't give me the space to clear my head, so I attempt to step back from him again. His arms tighten around me again.

"You owe me something, love," he announces with a small grin.

"I didn't know I borrowed something from you," I tease, knowing exactly what he's talking about. The kiss that I wiped away, as if it is that easy to get rid of his touch.

His head dips and reclaims my mouth in much the same way he did only a few minutes ago. I have the same reactions; rise to bat shit crazy mode with my head dropping between my shoulders and desire wreaking havoc on every cell within. If Milani has ever felt this way for any guy that she met, kissed, screwed, then threw away in the same day, then I completely understand why she did it. Giving half the chance, I would do all of it with Robert, but pitching him out with the trash is just not an option. You don't throw treasure away to be collected and treasured by someone else.

I wrench my mouth away from Robert's and turn my face, with barely any common sense residing in my head. "You have to stop doing that Robert, or Travis is a dead man no questions about it," I groan against his clean-shaven jaw.

He chuckles softly against mine, igniting sensations under my flesh again. "Okay, but I need to do that again before you go back with Travis. You've gotten to me, Trinity. If I'd never touched you, you wouldn't have, and we need to talk after this is over before I make you're mine completely."

I was yours before it ever began, and we should've talked four years ago.

Of course, I can't say that, or Travis' probably still a dead man. "Okay, where do you want me to meet you?"

For one last kiss, I'll move heaven, earth, and Travis out of the way at the same time. If Travis catches us in the act of saying goodbye, so be it. I sort of hope that he does catch us because I won't have to leave Robert at all.

"In my bedroom as soon as the meeting's over. I've wanted to touch you like this since we collided in the kitchen this morning… but not through you clothes. We need much more privacy than the living room allows."

Janine picks that time to insist *'I need you to hold me'* in lyrical form over our heads from an unseen surround system. She's putting words to my emotions and towing me deeper into Robert's orbit with every forward beat of the slow-moving melody moving throughout the room.

"Only if you promise to hold me for at least ten minutes," I demand, while placing the side of my face against his chest.

I listen to the humor reverberate under his shirt and out of his mouth, along with his heartbeat.

"Twenty minutes and you have a deal, Trinity. Any longer than that, baby, and this sting will be over with before it even begins."

Sting? More cop talk.

Something tells me not to mention it though. "Are we really negotiating how long we'll touch, Robert?"

"We have to or somebody will die today and that's a promise."

I snort, which makes him laugh out loud. "Okay, let's call time on this touching session and then we'll start another soon. I need to clear my head of you."

"Fine, Dr. Moody, I'll give you space, but I'll see you soon too to take back the space I lost in your head."

"You better," I whisper, as the music and humor fade away together.

I struggle to retract my hands from his body, then not look deeply into his dark eyes. They're magnets for me, since the moment when I ran into him at the coffee shop. When I first realized he could be more than a father figure to me, someone special that I knew to keep my distance from.

It's too late for that now, as his head dips so he can kiss the side of my mouth. Miguel's hit record *Sure Thing* begins to play. Robert knew better than to kiss me full on. Then he's gone, like the breeze slipping through my fingers.

"In the kitchen, sweetheart," he commands softly on his way out of the room.

My feet stay glued to the spot as I watch his retreating backside vanish. The back of him is not a sight I plan to get used to. Travis is going down fast if I have to set him up myself.

The things we do for love, I groan in my head.

It takes two seconds for my own random thought to knock me completely off kilter.

"Ah shit, I love him," I say under my breath, letting my head drop back onto my shoulders to stare at the vaulted ceiling with a fan spinning lazily above my head.

"Why are you groaning and staring at the ceiling when you need to be in the kitchen?" Milani snaps.

My head wrenches upright, letting my eyes roam over her leaning around the doorway, while eating a sandwich and dropping crumbs on the floor.

"Chick, you're just as nosy as Paisley… and you just *ate*, Milani. You and Jaden are going to be big as two houses."

"And you'll tell my fat ass to get in the gym while you babysit Jaden's fat ass. See, it's all worked out. Now, get your fine ass that I'll be jealous of after I give birth in here and let's get Operation Disturbing underway so you can be where you want to be." She smiles deviously.

Yep, she heard me when I said I loved her father. I follow her into the kitchen. David, Jamal, Rasheed, and Rhys are gathered around the island identical in looks and position to Milani's. Who the Seth?

I'll be sure to ask Robert when we're having our own side meeting in his bedroom. Although, he seems to like to keep things hidden. Probably has good reasons too. I'll try to honor most of them, until I can't.

Paisley and Milani sit at opposite ends of the island on black-leather cushioned stools, with Rhys and Rasheed on each side of their women. I approach Milani from the backside and stop at the corner of the countertop, perching my elbows on the hard surface. Robert looks across the surface, from his position in the middle. A spot for command that he looks comfortable in, in his element, making me think he's done this a million times before. He skims over the faces around him. But why would he do this a million times, unless he led teams before?

"What we're going to have to do to catch Travis in his shit isn't simple in the least, people. Trinity has to go home with him and live her everyday life. The plan is for the Travis to do the same and continue seeking out suppliers, or at least thinks he has to until the end of the week when I have everything in place for his fall as up and coming kingpin of Miami, so no heroics, Trinity. Go to work. Play wifey at home. No sneaking through Travis' things looking for evidence. We'll do the dirty work."

He turns to two of the men standing side by side. "Jamal and David, you're on surveillance with two targets; Travis and his main lieutenant Blair, who we'll hope rats on Travis since he does Travis' dirty work but seems to be the weakest link at this point. He seems to know the most about Travis' operation. The backgrounds I had run on Owen and Shane comes in soon. Jamal, you cover Blair. You won't look suspicious in his neck of the woods. Get as many pictures as you can of him going in and out of pharmacies, trying to extort the business owners. David, since you're a white guy, Travis is your priority, and I'll have more guys for surveillance rotation by the end week for the both of you. My people should already be on the other two goons, Owen and Shane."

"Paisley, you call Trinity as you usually would—"

"Which is almost every day," she interrupts. "So that's simple."

Rasheed smiles at her.

Robert looks sternly at them both. "Make it *every* day, Paisley, but ask a key question every time, 'has her day has been as long as yours?' That means has anything changed on the home front. If she says yes…" He turns to me. "That means you need to get out right then, and that's what you do no matter what's going on even if it's nothing. Bad feelings are warnings that should never be ignored. You're somewhere you shouldn't be if you get them."

"Amen on that," Milani chirps while raising her hand, with personal experience and a bullet graze from what happens when you ignore your instincts.

Rhys snickers. She glares at him.

"Getting shot is still not funny to me to, Rhys, and you'll pay for laughing tonight," she warns.

"Whatever you're charging, I'll pay happily," Rhys replies.

He rarely talks loud. People who are prepared to show and prove don't.

Robert cuffs Milani's shoulder with one hand. "I'll have a guy sitting point somewhere outside your house day and night to pick you up, Trinity, right at your front door. It'll be different guys in different cars, so Travis doesn't start to wonder why the same person's sitting outside his house. You don't worry about who'll pick you up. All the guys are trusted associates of mine, but don't take unnecessary looks, long or short, out the window trying to find them. If you say yes to Paisley at any time about your day, she'll text them yes. If you can't get out in thirty seconds, they'll come to you, so don't panic. If this operation lasts longer than a week, we'll acquire a safe house nearby. I'll have Milani text you the address like it's her new address."

His head swivels to Milani. "Your job is not to worry about any of—"

"Not going to happen, daddy," she cuts in. "I'm calling Trinity every hour on the hour."

Robert shoots her a harsh frown too.

She glares back. "Don't look at me like that, daddy. She's one of the sisters you never gave me and I'll worry. I'm calling you right after I call her, as a matter of fact."

"Baby girl, you don't want to make Travis suspicious do you? We don't know how dangerous he is or what he'll be keeping tabs on concerning Trinity. He's not stupid. You could put him on our scent by simply acting out of the ordinary and give him a single reason to be even more suspicious of Trinity and ruin everything."

Milani huffs air then bites into her sandwich while giving him the evil eye. "Fine. I'll call ten times a day instead of twelve."

"Make it three, one for each part of the day. Time your calls so they last for different intervals but takes place an hour later than the last time you called the day before so she's not in the same place every time you call. False labor's a good excuse to keep calling your girl up at any time of the day or night. Trinity will have reason to be looking for your call and need thirty minutes to calm you down, three hours the next time. Fake a Braxton-Hicks episode tomorrow at the airport, so he doesn't get nervous when you call in the middle of the night. If we start getting predictable, we could all die fast."

That truth serves a healthy wallop of trepidation. I get cold feet. This operation needs a time frame. I don't plan on walking on eggshells around Travis for forever.

"If this isn't over in one month, I'm out," I announce.

Robert nods. "This will last two weeks at the most, Trinity, or we'll call this operation a bust and let the local authorities know who they need to start paying close attention to if they're not onto him by then. Travis will get cocky once his plans start to come together and make some mistakes that should easily lead back to him. We're just trying to rush that along, not be heroes."

Two words stick out in my mind; local authorities.

Who are we working with now?

I don't get the opportunity to ask, because Rhys clears his throat first. "What do you need me to do?"

Only then do I realize what Rhys could go through if he's a part of Operation Disturbing, and guilt ripples through me like a tsunami. "Oh God, Rhys, I didn't think about what this investigation would do to you, or wanted it to involve you or Milani, especially not with the baby on the way. Travis' goons will constantly remind you of Madeleine's death. I should just leave this alone and report what I know to the cops, then dump Travis' ass."

Rhys' expression dulls. "No, I'm going to do this and I promise that Milani, the baby, and I will be okay. This'll just be more justice for

Madeleine." Then he smiles. "I swear Milani's strong enough for the both of us, and you'll get to counsel us if we have any ill-effects from this investigation."

Milani harrumphs. "That'll help you to deal with any ill-effects that you may have from taking down your boyfriend too, Trinity. You know you love to talk and coach people through their lives."

I sigh. "I do and that's why I love my job, but…"

Why couldn't I save Taylor with my ability to coach others through their life? It's all I ever wanted to do, although Taylor probably wouldn't have needed it. He would've lived a good life as a good man.

I get that odd punch in the heart, wait for the inevitable tears to come. Robert walks over to lug me to my feet then into his arms, staunching the incoming emotional overload dead in its path. I submerge my head in his chest, fisting the material at his waist.

He whispers against me ear, "You weren't supposed to save Taylor, Trinity. You were thirteen-years-old, and it was your parents' job to save you both, but no one's perfect and some things we learn the hard way when it comes to raising kids. At least, your parents moved away from the east side before they lost you too. You're still here, so they did something right."

Apparently, I've been thinking out loud again. "I don't resent them for not moving away in time, Robert."

"No, you resent yourself for being right next to him when it happened and not being able to prevent his death, which has left you feeling helpless, but you're not. You do something each time you've tried to help someone out of a bad situation that you've come across for as long as I've known you. I watched you try to make the wrongs you've encountered right, the very same reason why we're all in here now. This is your calling, love, but you have to remember life doesn't teach us lessons in the ways we'd like to learn them. Life makes sure they'll stick. You lost a brother and your parents lost a child. Trust me, neither you nor your parents will forget that lesson without the help of Alzheimer's or stray away from what you're supposed to be doing unless you're a vegetable."

No one ever explained it to me like that before, I could never get pass my grief to the root of my own emotional issues, which is why I always need to control something. Robert's at the right age to be able to hit on my problem and say the right words that make so many other things better. I know what I could and should do for the Taylor Moody's that are still left in this world, and the stupid tears start to roll anyway, quietly and soaking the front of Robert's shirt. Cleansing. I'm starting to finally really grieve Taylor, and let him go.

Robert pulls me even deeper into his embrace, and begins to run his hands up and down my spine. "Rhys, you have combat training, but you have a family now, so you'll be on call if we need to extract Trinity. I don't think we'll have to, but nothing except death and taxes is a sure thing. Milani will need security since she's close to everyone here in some way and can be used as a pawn in Travis' game if he feels we're getting too close. You shouldn't leave her alone unless I have someone to replace you before you go back to Miami. When you arrive, if I text you a strange number and name, it'll be a street address in Miami. Put it in your gps system, get there on the double, armed, and ready for combat. It'll be a war zone that I call you to."

Robert pauses for a moment. I can feel when his head dips and eyes start to drill into my back, like he's checking on me, but I'm fine miraculously and cried out already. I'm simply taking the chance to hold him because I've cried for Taylor for twelve years—not many more tears were left to spill. But am I going to tell Robert that I'm okay? No damn way.

Everyone else in this world has seized their chance to be trifling at some point, and I'm taking mine by playing the grief-stricken counselor that needs to be held until Robert and I are alone in his bedroom. I want to get there as fast as possible, and being in his arms is just as addicting as his touch. I'm hooked, and determined to get my fill of my chosen drug or rather of the drug that chose me, while he continues to address everyone.

"Rasheed, you're backup and on listening-duty at all times. Keep your police scanner close until I have someone to rotate with you too. Any strange calls with addresses that are connected to where anyone in this room works, lives, or have family are top priority. All addresses will be sent through an encrypted email to you and your replacement at all hours, including the address to places that Travis and his lieutenants are at for any reason. Get there if you hear them on the scanner and find out what the hell's going on, then report to me ASAP. Keep an ear to the ground with the local authorities as well. Most are them are crooked as hell, but Detective Williams and Stanford are good people, if not a bit dense sometimes and hard as hell of hearing. Ask for them personally if there's any need to contact the cops, people. Go nowhere besides work and home if you can help it. I'm not taking any chances with Travis, and no surprises will make sure this operation goes smoothly. Everyone who leaves at the normal time tomorrow will, and everybody, for God's sake, act like you normally would. Most of my precautions will already be in place here and in Miami by in the morning, so you are relatively safe. Don't discuss anything about this operation on open lines, but I'll be recording my conversations with Travis on my regular number for evidence. I'll line up black burners for everyone but Trinity, when we all get back to Miami. Now, I need to talk to Trinity to prepare her for a few things that she may have to deal with at home with Travis. Meeting over."

Only then do I let him go enough to allow him to guide us to the downstairs master's bedroom, hand in hand. I keep my chin tucked into my chest to hide my smile. I'm starting to like being trifling. It's not as bad as I thought it was.

CHAPTER 9

After the door closes behind us, *Pushin' Inside You* by Sons of Funk begins streaming through the speakers. He tugs me into his arms. I get just a glimpse of the California King bed decked out in a black and brown safari-print comforter and pillows of every size in front of me, two brown padded tall-back chairs that sit across from each other against walls on each side of the bed. Closed French doors with sheer curtains and an ordinary patio set on the balcony cease to exist when his body swallows mine.

"Trinity, sweetheart. It's okay. Taylor's in no pain and—"

I wrap my arms around his waist and lift my head with the small smile growing wider as he stares down at me worriedly, and that's all it takes to cut him off. "I'm good, Robert."

"You are?"

I prop my chin in his chest. "Yes. You've permanently fixed my problem with a few well-chosen words that I would've heard a long time ago if anyone had as much wisdom as you do."

His small smile shows up, and starts to grow. "*I've* fixed you, huh? I didn't know there was anything wrong with you."

"There was," I confess before letting my smile slip away. "I hid it well from everyone, and you did fix me, by telling me that if I was supposed to help Taylor, I would've if I'd been able to. What does a thirteen-year-old kid from the hood know about bullet wounds and CPR? But if I implemented a program like that in one of my parents' centers that gives everyone basic knowledge of medical training, do you know how many kids will still be alive when professional medical help finally arrives on their block?"

He sobers. "I have a good idea how many, most of them probably, but not everyone's going to be saved Trinity no matter what you do, as much as we'd like to believe that."

"I can accept that now, but it is hell to reconcile with failure when just one life you'd give yours for slips through your fingers, Robert."

"I understand where you're coming from, and I'll help as much as I can to get your program up and running, but that'll come in time and I still need to teach you basic self-defense moves before you go home now. I don't want you feeling helpless again."

"Fortunately, I'm not helpless when it comes to self-defense or we wouldn't be having this conversation."

Robert's facial expression hardens suddenly, almost to the point of scaring the hell out of me. I've never seen anyone so damn angry.

"What did Travis do to your hand in Milani's kitchen, Trinity? Because I'm going to do it to his when I catch him red-handed in pill-pushing right before I make sure he gets to where he belongs. I'm not talking about Club Fed either, but the roughest prison in the states for the rest of his life."

I lay my head in his chest, wallowing in the protective layer that Robert doesn't even know he's covered me in. However, Travis saw it in the kitchen before I felt it, when he couldn't be bothered to move so I could deliver the second load of Milani's baby gifts. When he decided that Robert was threat to our relationship.

"What he was doing was trying to establish control by squeezing my hand and relaying the threat that things would get worse for me if I agreed to this meeting with you and Milani. I don't even know if he realized he was doing that, but he knows there's something between us and he didn't hurt me like you think, just gave me my first real life lesson on abusive men. Textbooks only record the process and deaths. I gave him a lesson on strong black women with nails shaped like claws. The skin on his hand and wrist got a lesson too; its owner is *stupid*. Travis got the point that I can't be controlled by him, and I'm here."

Robert's chest begins to rebound against my cheek. I don't have to look up to know he's laughing quietly.

"Remind me not to try something like that with you. What do you know about self-defense?"

"I take classes at one of my parent's centers with a self-defense program for women whenever I can. They even have an annual tournament where we get to beat the hell out of men that volunteer and pay dearly for the privilege to see women in black Lycra boy shorts and tight T-shirts. Some of us have some class and wear longer shorts and looser tees. I'm not one of them though."

Robert's hands skim around my jaw before clutching it gently between his palms, lifting my eyes to his. His fingers rub against my skin like he's savoring the feel of it. His touch still has a side effect though; it's driving me nuts again.

"Robert," I moan, closing my eyes before his lips trespass against mine.

My mouth opens beneath his. His tongue tentatively strokes the tip of mine, and gives me a front row seat to what it means to been driven wild. Desire streaks through every cell of me. Holding me for twenty minutes isn't going to get rid of any of it or satisfy me. I step back out of his hold and reach behind my neck for the small button that fastens the loop of my sarong.

"We need to negotiate, Robert," I say quietly.

His nostrils flare. "If we do, what do I get for letting you change the terms of the deal?"

"Me." I jerk the button out of its slot.

He shakes his head and backs toward a tall-back chair on his right. "Not enough, love. I'll get stuck with whatever memory of your body you leave me with and my hand to replace your actual warmth for however long it takes to take Travis down. You'll have to make this worth my while."

I grin. My sarong hits the floor, pooling at my feet and leaving me in only the tiny excuse for panties that have been and still are being drenched with my need for him. I strike what I hope is a seductive pose of simply standing still with my hands by my side. "Just tell me what you want."

He moves the chair to the open midpoint of the foot of the bed and the door then stalks behind me. I don't look back, liking the mystery he's weaving with his unseen movements around the room. They only serve to increase the wetness pooling between my thighs, and then I hear the click of an object being placed down on a hard surface. Sons of Funk stop in mid high note, then start over from the beginning. The sensual and slow melody begins to make the atmosphere even thicker and harder to breathe by voicing what my body wants, for Robert to push inside of me.

"I take it you like this song, Robert."

"You take it right, Trinity, although you're too young to know about 1997, when music was still understandable and singers could hold a note. Your generation needs a bucket to carry a tune, and this'll be your song too before this memory's done being made."

I find no reason to argue with him about anything, especially if he's going to give me what I want, what I hope we both want, while I wait for him to come up behind me and touch me. He doesn't, but walks around me instead and stands in front of the chair.

I snort. "A lap dance? Is that all you want?"

A lap dance is cake for any woman with rhythm in her hips and a lap to grind on. Robert will be my slave before this is all over.

He grins. "A lap dance's too cliché for criminals with fast money.

No, you're going to make love to me while I sit, and we'll see if you can keep quiet while doing it. If you can, I'll let you cum before I do. If you can't..." He shrugs. "Well, I guess you'll have to try again when Travis is no longer an obstacle for us, and we'll both suffer with blue balls until he isn't."

I don't relish suffering with a blue anything, and cock an eyebrow. "You're not going to cum either if I can't be quiet?"

I'm finding it hard to believe that he'll deny himself release if I lose, which makes us both losers when he doesn't have to be one.

He's more man than I thought he was. How is that even possible?

He pulls his shirt out of his khakis and hauls it over his head, while toeing his shoes off by stepping on the heels of them, kicking them under the chair. Enormous muscles ripple in his arms and chest like waves coming in and going out to sea. I caress the side of my mouth to make sure I'm not drooling—that wouldn't be classy of me either—as he shirt drops to the floor in front of him.

"That's right, Trinity. You have to satisfy both of us with little help from me or we both don't finish. The first moan out of your mouth is the end of our time together for now and you get no kiss goodbye."

What a fucking challenge! I can't make anybody a slave like this.

"Can we at least get on the bed?" I yelp.

"Nope, too easy for you. You'll be able to balance and fuck my brains out with no problem over there," he responds nonchalantly, while I watch him tow his belt and pants open, down his thighs built like trunks made of the smoothest bark and darkest chocolate.

The limb pushing against his black briefs hugging his legs like lovers isn't made like the average branch either. It curves up his thigh and rests under his mid-section along his waist. My mouth drops open. The challenge just doubled. I don't see how I'll be able to fit all of him inside me. Even if I split his length in half and distribute it between both sets of my lips, there'll still be some left over to extend from both of my fists.

"Robert—"

"Are you afraid of me, Trinity?" he asks in a gentle tone, with a little bit of worry interwoven through it.

"No, but you're a man with two different thinking heads, and one usually has more control than the other does. You might not even realize you're impaling my lungs until it has collapsed around your penis."

He roars with laughter. "Both heads want you, Trinity, and—"

"I can tell," I yelp. This is a problem that I'll literally have to face *head* on or bow out of ungracefully. I don't do ungracefully.

"*And* neither one us will hurt you if I can help it. I'll tell you what. If you hurt yourself, I'll make it better and make you cum only, before you leave me with only my hand and the memory of you to carry me throughout the rest of my days, even after Travis is gone."

I start to melt inside at his promise that I'll be the last woman in his life if he hurts me, but I'm no fool. What I'll be is the last blood relative to carry my father's name in a long line of Bookers too if Robert skewers through my uterus. My core begins to throb and my mouth salivates, as if both are communicating they'd really like to take that chance and have no sense of self-preservation whatsoever.

"Are you using reverse psychology on my body? Because it's working," I admit.

Too damn well! But if I take him inside, I'll hurt more than me. I'll hurt my grandmother and my mother in between us.

He cocks one side of his mouth. "No, I'm not psyching you out. That's why you'll be making love to *me* and have all the control. I'm not the one to ever hurt you ever like this or want you to miss out on the opportunity to make love with me before you go home where Travis has all the opportunities and space to win you back, so go slow with me."

His chivalrous side just keeps getting bigger and bigger. He'll have me as *his* willing slave in no time if he keeps this up, and I haven't let challenges stop me before now. Every moment in my life has been a test so far, and I've managed to come out on top.

And somebody needs to learn that there won't be any more Travis and me.

"You need to stop talking, Robert," I demand, as I begin an unhurried and surefooted walk over to him. "You're wasting time."

He sits down just as I stop in front of him before bending over so my lips can connect with his, forming an airtight seal, before he can respond, by sliding his hands up my thighs. I shiver when a blast of heat follows the path his hands take to the skinny straps of my underwear resting high on my hips. His fingers tunnel under them, and begin to push my panties south. When they hit the floor, all hell breaks loose between my thighs. Sensations rip and collide with each other within me—impatience, craving to connect with him on a carnal level, and an all-consuming desire to make Robert mine in every way. Nothing about making love with him will be slow.

My palms drop to his thighs. He shudders and breaks the connection of our mouths to gasp for air. I smile at my effect on him, and I'm only touching his legs through his briefs that have to go. My hands slide up his thighs, trailing over the lump of velvet steel threatening to come out the top of his waistband. He curses. I smile then send my fingertips on a voyage beneath the gray trim of his briefs. He rocks back in the chair then balances on its back legs and lifts his hips so I send his underwear on the same path as mine.

I have to gasp as twelve inches of penis covered in a hardened black coffee-hue makes an appearance. Do I have doubts that Robert will hurt me as I stare at his more than impressive manhood and skim his underwear down his calf muscles that make Olympic-trained runners look sickly?

No.

Do I have several doubts that I'll hurt myself?

Damn skippy! I'll try to take every inch of him inside. My center is demanding that I do, or suffer the consequences; live with the knowledge that I wasted an opportunity to do as much as with Robert as I possibly can before I go home.

He drops the chair back on all four legs. I'm not sure if my womanhood or throat is twelve inches long, but I'm about to find out. Then I drop to my knees and take his length in both hands before lowering my head. Robert hisses above me before I've buried the tip of him between my lips and hollowed out my jaws. He curses and his hands take up resident on each side of my head. I wish I could let my hair down to add a little more sexiness to my appearance as my head begins to bob and sink, working him inside my mouth one inch at a time.

"Shit, Trinity, if you keep that up, the only thing I'll have been inside is your lips," he warns through his gritted teeth before I've covered six inches of him in my mouth's juices.

My head dives upwards, emptying my mouth of him or he won't understand a word I'm about to say. "I'm not done yet. I still have half of you to go."

"That's the half that'll make this a done deal for me, so up, sweetheart."

"I don't like orders, Robert," I mention with one eyebrow raised and a small smile. "They make me want to do the opposite just for the hell of it." The apex between my slippery thighs pulses and makes me take notice of the juices trapped between them.

He grins, and slides his hand from my head to under my arms. "Not this time, love. Try me up when we have all day and night."

All day and *night?*

More fluids flood the space where my legs connect. I tremor, as he lifts me to my feet then slide his warm hands between the slits of my legs.

"Open, love, and come closer," he commands.

I more than like that order, relocate each foot on each side of the chair, with the part of my body that's starting to ache for him positioned in his face. "How athletic are you, Trinity?" he asks out of nowhere.

"Not as athletic as you obviously, but I make do in the bedroom while avoiding gyms like the plague."

He snorts. "Then lift your right leg over my shoulder." I snort this time, after I realize what he's about to do to me. It'll be over for me if he does.

"That's not nec—"

"Up, love. You know not to cum yet," he interrupts. I do know, but my body does its own thing, and Robert won't listen to me even if I waste the breath to tell him that. I can tell this by the rigid set of his jaw.

"I tried to warn you," I say before throwing my leg over the back of the chair and giving him a front seat to the very center of me that's shaved bare and will spew juices all over him before he can take cover.

"Duly noted, Trinity, now give me what I want," he growls low in his throat while spearing through me with his dark orbs. The pressure to cum right then mounts higher than it ever has before. It's like his wants are being dumped on the load of craving that I already carry, and he's unloading just by looking at me, which influences me to do anything he wants me to. His head swoops down and submerges itself in the opening of my thighs. I grab for his shoulders as my knees go weak before his tongue begins to lap at everything between my southbound lips. The urge to moan loud and long overtakes me. I recall I can't do that then cover

143

my mouth with one hand and thrust my hips in any direction that leads away from his mouth.

His hands slide to the globes of my ass and push me forward again so he can apply suction to the tiny nub already extending beyond my southbound lips at this point. Waves of pleasure rip through my torso, and I jerk backwards trying to escape them and him before I reach the inevitable conclusion; climaxing all over him literally.

"Jesus Robert, you have to stop. I don't have orgasms like normal women," I caution.

"So you squirt, huh? And I didn't say I wasn't going to try and make you cum, Trinity. I said not to make a sound," he taunts and commences with submerging his head and feasting on me.

I start to shake badly, and moan in my head as the world blurs before my eyes. Denying my body release is actually costing me control over it big time.

"Let go, sweetheart," he says suddenly between my thighs that are muffling his words, but I understood him and do as he says.

Physical pleasure begins to spray into his chest. Extreme ecstasy takes me my foot from under me. It's bad enough I only had one working in the first place. Robert guides me down his front, the direction my body was headed in anyway, while clutching two handfuls of my rear in both hands until I sit in his lap, with the hard ridge of his manhood smashed under me and lying along the slit of my behind. The impulse to grind on him takes over. I hope doing that will dull the bliss that's ripping through and out of me and last for minutes sometimes, but I only provoke another orgasm to erupt like an angry geyser from me.

I rush forward; smashing the droplets of juices laying on his chest between us and wrap my trembling arms around his shoulders, holding on for dear life as my awareness of the world around me rushes away until I'm reduced to basic instinct and barely aware of Robert rocking back and forth beneath me. He slides his length along my body, grazing my clitoris in the process and sending aftershocks through me, which manifests as little showers that leave my body sporadically while he plants tiny kisses on the side of my mouth. When my body simmers down finally, I've buried my face in his neck, and prayed ten times that I'll survive this second meeting with him. I won't, if he doesn't stop moving.

"Robert, for God's sake be still," I whisper with my hands buried in his hair at the nape of his neck.

"You started it," he whispers back with a chuckle. "Okay, now?" I shake my head. "Well, love, you'll have to be because this isn't over yet. I still need to be inside you, and you still have to be quiet until after I cum, or I don't get to."

I giggle. "That's a serious load of responsibility you're laying on my shoulders, love."

"Yes it is and I feel no shame about doing it. Now lift your fine ass so you can make it mine, Trinity."

I sit up, look directly in his eyes that are glazed in a thick coat of yearning then clutch his face between my hands before getting to my feet. He palms his penis and stands it up like a missile ready to fire off while he grips one of my thighs. Before my nerves can go bad and I start to doubt if I can take all of him, I lower myself. He glides through my opening that closes tightly around his tip, then exhales heavily and drops his head back on his shoulders, his long dreads falling behind the chair and out of sight.

I bite my lip to keep from crying out, as he stretches my walls beyond their limits and more earth-moving sensations explode within. None of them are pain, but the bliss, erupting like an active volcano and bouncing off the walls of my channel, is too much. I start to hyperventilate and sit all the way on his lap just to stop the angry mob of vibrations from coursing through me.

"Shit, Trinity, you weren't supposed to take all of me inside me. That's a lot of heat and wetness you're torturing me with. I don't think I've ever been this deep inside anyone before, and I'm only so much man. You have to move, love, or I'll start to fuck you at warp speed."

"You're a big boy. You can handle it," I taunt breathlessly then rise up.

Only two inches of him have been excavated before my body demands that I take him back inside, not wanting any amount of space between us. When I feel the tip of him skim the edge of my cervix, the contact with the thickness of his head sends a shower of pure joy through me and makes him grunt softly, and then his fingers dig into my hips like they've found a much needed lifeline. He starts to chew on his bottom lip while looking me straight in the eyes. I begin to revel in making him the one who has to keep quiet, as I rise and sink downward again while tightening my out-of-shape muscles that act as a vise grip and walls to keep him imprisoned.

At this moment, I'm so proud of my walls *and* the swollen nub that's stationed above the mouth between my thighs. Both rarely give me this much control in the bedroom, too sensitive to be touched when I'm sexually activated. It's absolutely fulfilling to be the one to give pleasure as I get to ride a man earnestly, creating a friction so devastating I should already be a limp noodle and cumming all over the place by now. But I want to see what his face looks like in the throes of bliss and his eyes, which are filled up with angst from the exquisite torment cause by sliding against the soft tissue inside me that is wet, ultrasensitive, and craving every available inch of him for as long as I can have him.

I discover that it's utterly satisfying to be able to drive someone out of their mind until they don't know if they're going or coming, until they cum for me, and cum for me is what he's going to do. First, I brace my hands on his shoulders then increase my climb to a few more inches higher along his length, so it takes me twice as long to drop to his lap. The pleasure triples, making me bite my lip to keep from telling him that it has. He closes his eyes and starts to blindly guide my hips in a faster tempo that has left behind the slow tune playing above our heads, while angling my body in different slants so he enters me in positions that hit every pleasure zone in the area.

Suddenly, I'm no longer in control of what my body does to his. His hips start to rise and hurtle into the backs of my thighs when I drop down. The flesh-to-flesh contact and setting of the pace at his insistence is my undoing—I'm back to being the one on the receiving end of too much pleasure to tolerate, my eyes rolling back in my head, and digging my nails in his shoulders to seek my own lifeline. It seems that lost of control ramps up my body's sensitivity, and that makes sense since what we desire most in the world is the exact opposite of what turns us on in the bedroom.

Spirals of untainted joy undulate through me until I've lost all feeling in my head, my extremities in tight balls against his neck and the carpet, and a pool of my climax is flooding his lap. I bury my head in his neck. The orgasm makes me push my back outwards uncontrollably. Robert's arms glide under my thighs and lift my legs, which leaves my body at a forty five degree angle that gives Robert room to power drive into me like a train barreling down a track for what seems like forever while I smother my screams from bliss that's swamping me. At this point, I'm not sure who's riding who. Then he surges forward while pulling my hips toward him.

He enters me at maximum speed and plunges deep before he buries his head in my chest, and starts to curse a blue streak while shuddering beneath me with his arms wrapped around my back. When he stops shaking and filling my tunnel with his essence, he loosens his arms around me and exhumes his face from my skin while gasping for air. I sit up, after finding half of my right mind along with a few of my fine-motor skills. He looks down at his soaked lap then smiles at me. I frown.

"Don't be embarrassed about having the gift to cum with your whole body, Trinity. Most women would kill you for the ability, and I don't have to wonder if I'm satisfying you. You're one hell of a woman and Travis was a fool to ever let you take your heart back from him."

I tilt my head to the side. "He never had it, but you do," I confess quietly.

He frowns then digs his fingertips into my waist almost to the point of hurting me. "Do I? Hold on to it love, until we talk about what kind of future we'll have together."

I start to think that Robert might not be the man for me because he doesn't want to be, and we're just ships passing in the night. That would be fine for me if it was any other man, but none of them have ever affected me like Robert does, so I'm not fine. And therein lay another problem. I've never wanted my heart to be broken, but it breaks away from my chest and plummets into my stomach anyway. The back of my eyes begin to burn.

Oh no you won't start this 'crying over a man' shit now, Trinity, especially not while he's looking at you.

I find a spot over Robert's head to look at instead of the worried expression in his face. Then I inhale deeply, trying to patch up the hole in my chest where my heart used to be until I can at least get to my shower, my rock solid composure a thing of the past. I don't want to be composed. I *want* to cry, but I don't.

"So is this just a hook up or a cutty-buddy thing where we get together when we can?" I ask, unable to look at him.

His hands rise and ensnare my cheeks between them before turning my face to his, his eyes settling deep into mine. "Trinity, you deserve better than either of those, and no, I don't want that with you, which is why you shouldn't be considering a life with me either. I have twenty years on you, and will be using a cane when you're just entering your prime."

"Robert, I already know you treat your body like a temple," I argue. "You don't smoke, or drink and eat pork anymore since you move to Aruba."

"*Anymore*," he emphasizes with a sad smile, pulling a reluctant one from my lips. I definitely don't want to be smiling when I already know where this conversation's headed; me going in one direction, Robert in another.

"You're making my point for me, you know? When I enter my prime, you'll still be in yours, so don't push me away because of the age difference. I don't think I should've been trying to find what I want out of life with someone my age anyway. Who's ready to settle down at twenty-five besides me, oh and Milani? No one."

"You're too mature for your age, Trinity."

"That's my cross to bear, Robert, and yours is to say why you really don't want to be with me because mature people don't mince words, and I'll respect what you say. I think I deserve the truth and will nag or dig until I get it, but I'll never push myself on you, and will walk away gracefully."

"You don't have to walk away at all. I just want us to have an understanding and don't want you to regret settling down with me because I don't think I can do all the things that settling down requires anymore, like making babies." So that's why he's single.

"That's bullshit, Robert. Men still make babies at seventy. I don't think you *want* any more babies after what Jessica did to you with Milani. Maybe not even get married again." He nods. I nod too. "Finally, some truth from someone without me having to pull their teeth out."

"Trinity, I think you're one of those women that already know the truth without the teeth pulling. You just need proof of what you've already figured out for yourself."

"True, but I don't like to speculate, so Robert I'm going to make this easy for you and say Paisley was right before I say—"

"Paisley was right about what?" he cuts in softly.

"Who, you mean, and she was right about *you*. You're a beautiful mistake." Then I slide from his lap, and rescue my clothes from the floor.

"Trinity, wait," he urges, then sits up ramrod straight and lays his hands on his thighs.

I slip my dress over my head. "No waiting, Robert. Although I didn't say I wanted to marry and have babies with you right off, we both now that's what I'll want three or four years from now when I think I have you all figured out. I'm just glad you said something now before I got too deeply involved with you and spared us from our relationship going bad after the honeymoon phase is over. I'll walk away now like I promised, and I wish you the best. We're still friends, so no worries about how I'll act after today. I know things like that bother men after they're done having sex with a woman."

"It's *tonight*, Trinity, and dark outside. We've been in here for two hours, not twenty minutes, and I'm not your friend. I never was, but I can't go back to being a father figure in your life either."

I hadn't notice the time slipping away. It still feels like we've only been here for a few minutes, but I'm learning time with the one you love will never be long enough, and it's definitely time to go. "Trust me, what I've just done with you will never make me see you that way again, Robert, and I hope we can be friends, because I don't want to lose you in my life even if we can't have one together. But I don't regret what we've done, just that I didn't get a chance to ask who Seth is. I don't think you'll tell me anyway, and I'm more than capable of walking away from this phase in our life gracefully too."

He grimaces. "A *phase*, Trinity? And Seth's an acquaintance of mine that helps me out in situations like yours."

"A phase is all we can be, Robert. You just said so even if you didn't really say it, and tell Seth I said thank you for whatever help he provides in stopping Travis." I exit the room, with my drenched panties balled up in my hand.

My heart lays in the fetal position in my stomach, broken.

CHAPTER 10

Suddenly, I feel like a ton of bricks have been dropped on me. Walking away from him is almost impossible, but I manage to enter the kitchen, and find everyone that was here when I left. I try to school my face into a blank mask, making my emotions ball up in my throat and sit there like a rock. Milani turns around first with a huge smile on her face. Paisley grins, just before Milani cranes her neck to look behind me then her smile slips away as I walk past her.

She grabs my arm and hauls me back to her still seated on the wooden stool. "What did he do, Trinity? You should be giggling like a school girl with him right behind you smiling like a damn Cheshire cat."

I look at her. If I didn't, she would get suspicious. "He didn't do anything, Milani. Calm down before you cause the baby stress."

My eyes drift down to her stomach that's resting against the island. At this rate, I'll never have a child, and that epiphany just adds to the rock's mass in my throat. I choke up.

Paisley rushes over to me, with a sad tilt to one side of her lips. "It's over already, huh?"

"It never began, P. I'm going to take a shower and go to bed. I'll see you guys tomorrow at breakfast." Paisley wraps her arms around me, and holds me to her tightly, while Milani keeps a firm grasp on my arm.

Paisley begins to whisper, "If he doesn't want you, move on again, but if you stand still long enough, thirty more guys will stop by you. At least one will take your mind off of Mr. Elliot long enough for you to get over him, while you wait for the one that your heart's meant for. Us ordinary woman go through this every day. You'll be fine. I'll make sure of it."

I pat her back, as if she's the one that needs consoling, with everyone drilling holes into me with their eyes. "I'm fine, love." I lie. "We would've never worked out. There are just too many years and differences between us, but you were right. He *is* a beautiful mistake." One I would make again and again if I had the chance.

I kiss her on the cheek, do the same to Milani before prying my arm from her grip. She frowns at me. I grin at her, though my face feels like it's going to crack.

"Smile, love. Everything's good and you promised you wouldn't get upset about this. We're being adults about it, and you have to be one too. Now walk away, Milani. *I'm* going to."

Robert's presence swamps the room behind me. An invisible thread strum tightens between us, which needs to be snipped if I'm going to be able to look him in the eye again. That won't happen tonight because I don't know how to cut ties that lead to the heart, and I'm not sure if threads linking to an organ is breakable. If they aren't, I'll learn to live with them and carry my head high while doing. I know my worth. If Robert doesn't, that's too bad for him.

I make a getaway through the double back doors, across the lawns to the deck in the back of Milani's home. I go in her back doors silently. If my luck's good, Travis is asleep already or handling some kind of business on the phone, any kind of business, as long as he's not asking me a million questions. After bypassing the kitchen, I glance into the living room, find it empty, and let a bulky coat of annoyance settle over my skin before starting my climb up the steps slowly. At the top of them, I discover the door to the guest bedroom I share with Travis is closed, hopefully locked. Then I'll have an excuse to sleep anywhere but in the same bed with him.

However, my luck hasn't been good with men today, and I'm pretty sure Travis has probably been waiting for me to get back before I even left with Milani in her new truck. I inhale deeply, readying myself for something like the Spanish Inquisition or Twenty Questions to take place as soon as I'm in the bedroom. I turn the knob. The door opens. I walk inside the pitch black room, thinking maybe he isn't even here.

"Go shower, Trinity. I know that's where you're headed," he says suddenly, making me jump three feet in the air, land, and then clutch my chest with my free trembling hand. "We need to talk when you get out though, so don't take too long."

"We can talk now, Travis. Today has been a long day and I don't know if I'll make it back out of the shower tonight."

"If you don't come out, I'll come to you, and you don't want that."

I bristle. "What the hell does that mean?"

"You want nothing to do with me right now, so the last thing you want is me anywhere near your naked body. I'm trying to spare myself a case of blue balls. Just looking at you will give me that, unless you want—"

"No," I cut in before he can finish. This is one of those rare moments where I don't want to know what's going to be said next. "I'll bathe quick and then come talk to you, but talk quick because I'm tired."

"I'm sure you are," he comments dryly.

A small click emanates from his direction. Light illuminates the room. Now, I can see his face and the sarcastic expression to go with his tone as he sits on the bed with just his shorts on. I don't want to see anything concerning him, so I lope through the bathroom doorway before shutting and locking the door behind me. After flipping the light switch, I move between the sunken tub and sinks, to the small glass cubicle stationed in front of the toilet.

After opening the door and adjusting the shower to as hot as I can stand it, I strip the sarong off quickly, drop it and my underwear on the floor, and submerge under the spray. I want to sink to my knees and relieve my throat of the block of emotions, but Travis will want to know why I was crying. The red eyes and hoarse tone that comes with being an ugly crier will be a dead giveaway, so I wall the emotions up in a different place, my soul, and begin to bathe.

I start to develop a headache from the images of Robert pushing inside of me, while I soap my body then proceed to rub my skin raw hoping to relieve it of the memories from his touch, but I can't get Robert out of my head. I decide to just get out the shower and face the music that's playing on the other side of the door. How I wish it was the soulful tunes of my favorite R&B jam, *Genius* by R. Kelly, but the situation waiting for me calls for the suspenseful, creepy echoes of danger lying ahead. I brought this shit on myself by letting Robert get to me in every way possible.

I turn the water off and snatch a huge towel from the bar mounted on the wall between the stall and the toilet. After wrapping it around my body and shoving the loose end between my breast and the section of cloth lying flat against me, I grab my clothes off the floor and walk out of the bathroom. When I find the bedroom empty, I stop in the doorway, raise my face to the heavens, and thank whoever is having mercy on me, probably Taylor. Inside my suitcase that sits on a six-drawer dresser on the right side of the room under a window, is every stitch of clothing I brought to Aruba, including the sheer sleeveless white gown that leaves nothing to the imagination

Supposed to have been incentive for Travis to get our relationship back on the right track. Now, it's just the first thing I touch, too tired to scavenge for something that says 'I'm not in the mood'. I draw the gown over my head after pitching my sarong and underwear in the dirty clothes sack at the back of my suitcase.

Instead of going to find Travis and get that talk he wants to have out of the way, I move to the bed, pull the covers back, and snuggle deep under them. I'm tired enough for sleep to claim me right away, and so does a dream with Robert as the star. He's not in a chair but on an elevated bed, with silk black sheets and steps beside it, in a pitch black room that seems to have no walls. I have to walk through mist rising from the floor to get to him while dressed in a white, baby doll nightgown, but I couldn't care less about the location and the dirty air. The fact that we're together is all that matters. Yes, I know it's a dream, but I don't ever want to wake up.

When I have one foot on the bottom step of the bed, Robert slides across the sheets to me and hauls me up the rest of the way effortlessly. When I kneel in front of him, he slides his hands up my stomach, stopping at my breast before drawing one budding nipple into his mouth. Moisture seeps between my thighs. Craving rushes through me like a rampaging hurricane, and saps my strength. I moan and collapse over him, laying my hands on each broad shoulder to hold up my weight.

He guides me down to my back then spreads my legs apart before settling between them at eye level with my bare mound. His head dips between my legs and sensations fire off with every sweep of his tongue. An orgasm is just appearing on the horizon when I hear, "Wake up, Trinity. You need to remember who this thick luscious ass belongs to."

It takes me several minutes in my dream world to realize the demand came from outside of my head, not from Robert's mouth but Travis'. I panic and scour the misty room for him, not finding him anywhere. I know he's there with us though. Then the sweep of Robert's tongue sets fire to my insides and draws my attention. I forget about Travis, and work to coax the orgasm that was deterred from getting any further than the horizon towards me.

"I don't know what the hell I was thinking when I let making money get in the way of me keeping you happy, Trinity." Travis' voice draws my eyes to the misty room again.

He's still lurking unseen, and that worries me. If he's not here, where is he? Better yet, he could just shut the hell up during my wet dream, where Robert's pushing my bent legs toward my abdomen and locking them in place with his palms pressing down on the area behind my knees. The position leaves me open for his mouth to apply suction so intense to my clitoris I yell out. My body tenses up and I no longer have to coax the orgasm to me. It's already on me like a whirlwind and spinning me up into the middle of its tempest.

My eyes pop open as all hell breaks loose in my core. I grab for the nearest stationary object to keep my body tied to the earth as my climax tries to rocket me into space, which is the pillow under my head, covered in my loose hair strangely. I could've sworn I went to sleep with it still in a ponytail, but I can't worry about that now. I need to get through this orgasm that has my whole body in its grip.

"That's my girl," Travis says proudly from below me weirdly, with a smile in his tone, when I'm through cumming and need two tall drinks of water.

I look down, hoping I'm still dreaming and Travis hasn't just feasted on me like a man that hasn't eaten in weeks. My knees pushed toward my abdomen and locked in place are the first thing I see. Travis' smiling face looking back at me from between my thighs with his hands placed in the crooks of my knees is the next. Then his chin that's soaking wet with the proof of my orgasm appears in my confused vision, before his supporting hands disappear. My legs, wobbly even when lying down, collapse to the bed. He walks on his hands over me, planting one beside my head to brace his weight on. Before I can protest by asking what the hell is he doing taking advantage of me in my sleep, he reaches down and aims his penis for my slick opening and slides into me with the ease that comes with the lubricants that he's already set free.

I moan uncontrollably while he plants his free hand on my abdomen then he starts to pound into me without even bothering to raise my legs for deeper penetration. At this point, he doesn't need to. With Robert fresh on my brain and ten inches of Travis slamming through my already highly-stimulated walls, attacking pleasure zones just inside of my tunnel that have already been shaken and stirred, my body responds to Travis' lovemaking with no problem. It just wants release again. Doesn't matter that my mouth's shaped in the formation of no and my mind's screaming it.

I turn my face to the side, unable to look at him. Having Travis inside me feels so wrong to my heart, but he feels so damn good to my body. Even though my heart belongs to someone else, my legs lift to wrap around Travis' waist so he can sink deeper into me. My toes curl behind his slim backside. My fists ball into the sheets at my side, hoping to bear the sensations roiling through me. All I want to do is get off then get him off me. The sooner, the better, which means I need to push him over the edge. I tighten my walls until they're suffocating his pole that's spearing through me like its running back and forth for its life.

He gasps above me, "Fuck, yes! You're mine, Trinity. I own this ass, and I don't know what to do to keep from cumming in it."

Only if you knew that you're getting sloppy seconds, I think before Travis' hand is turning my face to his. There's an angry glare in his frostbitten eyes that are more gray than blue right now.

"*Look* at me, Trinity. Robert will never know that he needs to swirl his tongue around your clit and fuck the spot hard just at your opening to make you cum so hard you shake the damn bed."

Nope he doesn't know, but I shook a damn chair for him tonight though.

I'm definitely not going to say that. "Shut the fuck up, Travis, and just fuck me already," I snarl, hating him for taking advantage of my vulnerability in my sleep and feeling absolutely amazing while he's pushing inside of me.

I hate me for feeling as if I'm betraying a man that doesn't even want me.

Travis drops his hand on one side of my head then shoves so far up into me he batters my g-spot and a few other overly sensitive spots on his way in. A climax rips through me with no warning. I swear they're never just small ones, always catastrophic ones that threaten to shake my world right off its axis. He pumps into me three times, aggravating the waves of bullying bliss already stomping through me, and making them harsher than they would be if he had just kept his skinny ass still. Travis starts to cum, while my body acts out violently.

I tremble and moan softly until my orgasm fades away and Travis and the bed are coated in the remnants of it. He looks down at his dripping wet abdomen then grins at me. I growl like a damn animal and shove him to the dry side of the bed before scrambling to my feet, planning to hide in the bathroom for the rest of the night.

He starts to laugh. "You can run from me, Trinity," he yells when I'm halfway across the room, "but I'll always find you, and your body will always will respond no matter how angry you are with me."

"Shut! The! Hell! Up, you trifling bastard!" I slam the door in his face and lock it, before stripping again to take a hot bathe and think about what I've just done.

I've slept with two men in twenty four hours, but at least I'm on birth…

I come to a standstill in the middle of the bathroom as a horror beyond horrors washes over me.

Oh God, I forgot to take my birth control pill today.

Even missing one can mean an unplanned pregnancy, and I'll have no idea who the father is, which is why they caution people to use *two* methods of birth control. Neither one is one hundred percent effective alone.

Oh, how the mighty have damn fallen.

But the deed's done, and I'm still coated in Travis, outside and in, and I've never felt so dirty in all my life. I rip the gown over my head then toss it into the mosaic trashcan hard enough to make it rock off balance against the floor between the sinks and the doorway. I sit down on the edge of the tub in the middle of the floor with my feet dangling over the edge and start another bath.

This time, I need to sit in the water. Maybe I can soak Travis' seed away since I can't wash inside of me. I make a vow to never let him catch me vulnerable in my sleep again or go to bed without being fully clothed, then sink into the water while it's still running. When I turn the taps off, the faint echoes of someone pounding on something somewhere nearby reverberate through the bathroom. I look behind me at the closed door while straining to hear.

"She's fine and bathing," Travis yells. "Go the fuck away, David!"

I assume everyone heard the short argument between us. Since David's and Jamal's room is just across the landing, we were probably loud enough to disturb their sleep. I cringe when I consider they may have heard me sleeping with Travis while knowing I just slept with Robert, and then I sink far enough down into the water to wet every inch of hair below my neck that reaches my shoulders. Fortunately, it's freshly permed and all I have to do is dry it when I get out, but nothing would be wet at all if Travis had kept his hands to himself. Then someone starts pounding on the bathroom door.

"Go the fuck away, Travis!" I yell.

"It's not Travis. It's David. Are you okay, Trinity?"

I wonder how David got into the bedroom, certain that Travis didn't let him in it willingly. But David's pristine tan body packed with muscles on a six two frame under dirty-blond baby soft curls professionally cut in the shape of a bowl with grey eyes on an angelic face with a square jaw and cleft chin would've gotten him in one way or the other.

"I'm fine, David," I reply in a much lower tone. "Nothing's wrong." But everything's wrong.

"Then why are you shut up in the bathroom? I need to see your face,

Trinity. Did he hit you?"

"*No*," I and Travis both bellow together.

"I just need to see your face, Trinity, and then I'll go back to bed," David promises.

"Fine." I get out the tub and pad dripping wet to the door slowly, unlock it, and stick my face around it. "I'm good. Travis just doesn't know how to respect a woman when she's sleep and take his ass to sleep too, so I'm pissed, but I'm not hurt."

"I wouldn't hit you anyway, Trinity," Travis scoffs from the bed. "I love you too much for that, but you can tell Robert while you're up, David, that Trinity's *mine*."

I huff air at his sudden possessiveness that's getting on my last damn nerve.

David looks back at Travis. "If Robert wanted Trinity, she'd be next door and not over here, so let that shit go before you start something you can't finish."

I don't think David meant to hurt my feelings with his words, but he did. I slam the door shut in his face.

A perfectly behaved woman wouldn't have done that. I haven't been that woman in a while, and the brokenhearted woman on this side of the door wants to be alone so she can cry her heart out in peace about the unblemished truth in David's words. That's exactly what I do, until morning comes before I'm ready for it to. I've filled the tub with hot water six times and cooled it off with my tears just as many before I'm all cried out, and decide to bathe and go home.

Once I've gotten out and drained the tub, I quit the room the same way I did before; in only a towel. Travis is nowhere to be seen in the bedroom. I raise my face to the heavens once again, and thank whoever had mercy on me for the small miracle and my hair being completely dry so I don't have to waste time drying it. As soon as I trudge over to my suitcase to find something comfortable to fly home in, the bedroom door opens behind me. I don't have to look back to know it's Milani and Paisley coming in. Both chicks are loud and early risers.

"Thanks for pushing me off on your father and out of your bed so you could sleep with Rhys, Milani," Paisley says dryly on the way in.

"You're welcome, P," Milani chirps back, making Paisley snort.

I find a nude-colored lace bra and matching panties on top of my overstuffed suitcase then put them on quickly while my girls take a stand on each side of me.

"Want to talk, T?" Milani asks before she starts to rub my bare back.

"Nope, I just want to go home and get this operation over with, and then I'm moving the hell out of Miami."

"I take it you're not coming to Aruba for a fresh start?" Paisley inquires from the other side of me.

With the memories here? Uh huh. I excavate a thin white jumpsuit, with slits down my arms and legs that open up at the slightest movement. Genie cuffs wrap around my ankles and wrists. The suit frames my hour-glass shape and thick globes of my ass without actually being form-fitting, forcing men have to use their imagination. "Nope, Paisley, somewhere in between here and Aruba sounds nice though."

"Daddy's cooked—"

"I don't want breakfast, Milani," I say before she can finish—don't need any more memories connected with Robert either. This weekend's worth of them is too much already. "I'm going straight to the airport."

"I figured as much," Milani comments dryly.

"You know you're beautiful in a tragic sort of way today," Paisley mentions offhandedly, while I search through my suitcase for my toiletry bag. In it is a comb to run through the loose waves in my hair curtaining my shoulders.

But her statements is so ridiculous, I stop to stare at her. "What the hell does that even mean, Paisley?"

"That means you usually have the beautiful confident woman appeal working for you, but you have sadness that's surrounding you like a fog and adding to your beauty now. It's breathtaking and tragic, and pitiful that neither man in your life knows what a treasure they're letting walk away, but I know."

"And what novel did you read that out of, P?" Milani inquires sarcastically.

Paisley beams at us both. "The one that I'm writing. I decided to follow my dreams and do what I want to with my life. That's why all hell is going to break loose when I get home. My parents are going to be enraged, but so be it. If they love me, they'll stick by me. If they don't, I'll adopt new parents. Trinity can be my mother, and Mr. Elliot my father."

I should be excited that Paisley's taking my advice and embarking on a new journey that she wants to travel in life. Well, I am excited, but I have my own major issues weighing me down today, like having to go home with a psychopath that takes advantages of me when I'm sleep, gives me earth-shattering orgasms and possibly a baby, and may try to beat or kill me before the next two weeks are up.

Milani smirks. "And if she has a kid with my father, it'll my sibling and my kid's younger uncle or aunt. That's so damn ghetto."

Paisley points a finger at Milani. "But it happens, so get over it now."

"I didn't take my birth control pill yesterday," I say suddenly. "And Travis managed to screw me last night by coming onto me while I was sleep."

Both women's eyes grow big as dinner plates.

Milani's hand flies to her mouth. "What are you going to do if you're pregnant?"

I exhale and look down in my suitcase. "I really don't damn know, Milani. Haven't thought about it and hope to hell that isn't what happens." But if it does, there's no way I'm getting rid of it no matter who the father is. I want to be a mother.

At this point, it doesn't seem like I'll find the right man to father my child, so I guess it's good both men will be out of my life in the next nine months. After watching Jessica raise Milani, I know I can love my child enough for both parents.

"Well, you should think about it," Paisley advises.

"I have. I'm keeping it."

"What if it's psychotic like Travis, or a criminal like my father?" Milani whispers.

I turn to her. "I'm a behavior specialist, Milani. I think I can handle that, and psychotics and criminals are born to unsuspecting people every day. At least I have a heads up and some access to preventive behavior measures, but I need you guys to keep this quiet until I find out if I'm pregnant or not."

"What about your birth control?" Paisley asks in a shushed tone.

"I'm not taking it anymore. If I am pregnant, the hormones can hurt the baby. If I find out in six weeks that I'm not, then I'll start back on the pill."

Milani moves in closer to me. "What about knowing who the father is?"

"I'll do DNA testing after it's born."

Giggling erupts from Paisley. "I don't think that'll be necessary. The potential fathers are so different, this is the one time just looking at the baby will answer that question."

She's got a point there.

Milani shakes her head. "Well, sis, I'm here for you but don't sink any lower than this or they'll call you more trifling than I was, and *nobody* can get more trifling than the old me."

"Travis has you beat, Milani. Do you know he was eating me out like he hadn't eaten in days while I was sleep and smiling like a damn clown when I found him covered in my orgasm? I was dreaming about Robert while he was doing it."

"Well at least one of you is happy as hell today. Travis is still smiling like a damn clown and eating my father's breakfast at the table with the guys like he didn't ask David to pass a message to daddy about who you belong to."

I shake my head, and start to comb my hair. "Now that *is* trifling."

"Damn straight," Paisley adds then unearths lip gloss from my toiletry bag and shoves it at me.

I take it and shove the comb back inside, before applying a coat to my lips then hand it back to her. "Thank you, glam squad of one. I'm saying goodbye now, girls. I'm leaving."

"I hope you're not leaving without saying goodbye," Robert says suddenly from behind me.

I turn around slowly with all the function of wooden stick in my body. "Goodbye, Robert. Thank you for being a good host."

I whirl back around on my bare heels, and packed the clothes down in the suitcase. Milani and Paisley kiss me on each cheek then scurry from the room like mice. I don't know why. The conversation with

Robert is already over as far as I'm concerned.

"Is that all you're going to thank me for?"

At least I thought it was over. "Don't be slick, and there's nothing else to thank you for."

Unless I count the baby that he may have given me but certainly doesn't want and breaking my heart.

"Alright. Can I get a hug goodbye then?" he asks while his allure starts to suck all the air out of the room.

Intuition tells me he's walking closer and I need to vacate promptly before I beg him to keep me. I sling the flap of my suitcase over the clothes and zip it close.

"Trinity," he starts, while stopping beside me.

"Don't, Robert. Just let it go please."

"I never meant to hurt you."

"You didn't. I did this to myself. I knew you were off limits and I cross the boundaries anyway. This is just the consequences." And the repercussions may come in nine months, but they'll be good ones.

The kind a woman that's meant to be a mother has to suffer through though I may have to live through a short hell with Travis first. Well, there's an end in sight to my unhappiness. In the end, it'll all be worth it, and I won't let a man that doesn't value what I have to give him or the broken heart that I've given myself ruin it for me.

"I'll be fine." Then I spin to him, with a bright smile that's authentic and fake at the same time. "You know what, I *am* fine, and truly thank you for all that you've done and will do for me. I have to go, but I'll see you later. Goodbye."

I pick my bags up, stand on my tiptoes, and kiss Robert's cheek just like I would've done at the end of any other time we've spent together for Milani's sake. Then I leave without looking back, extract my phone from my purse to call a cab for a ride to the airport. Then I join the others downstairs with my head held high. I still can't control what happens to me, but I always choose to be the bigger person.

Riding on the plane with Travis puts that theory to the fire, after he decides he'll catch an early flight with me as well. Almost made me lose complete control over myself several times. He whispers in my ear the entire flight about what he wants to do to me in the airplane's restroom. I warn him I'm consider stuffing his ass out of a porthole. Doesn't help, so I dig deep for the strength to not stab him with my breakfast fork just to get him to shut the hell up. He arrives home in one piece. I don't emotionally.

CHAPTER NAME 11

A week later, back in Miami

"No, Paisley, my day hasn't been as long as yours, but it's getting there. I could barely find my desk after I came back from lunch. Travis sent twelve bouquets of different colored long-stemmed roses. The stupid delivery man put them *all* on my desk and ruined some referral paperwork that I was filling out for a client to see a psychiatrist. If I wake up one more time to Travis unzipping the jacket to my jogging suit, I'm going to say to hell with Operation Disturbing and just move into an extended stay hotel."

Rocking back in my office chair on the second floor of a three-story stucco building, I think about taking a power nap while Paisley cackles in my ear at Travis' exploits of a man trying to win back what he never had, my heart. The flowers reduce me to a sneezing fit first.

I never had allergies to flowers until today but not uncommon when I have a florist shop worth of vegetation in a thirteen by thirteen office filled with furniture that's leaving nowhere else for the multi-floral scents to go but up my nose. Two light blue couches create a calming atmosphere at the front of the room, along with the combination of fake floral arrangements in silver planters on oak sofa and end tables and hung scenic pictures that greet my clients when they open the door. The setting invites them to sit or lay while I observe and absorb their troubles from a matching arm chair placed between the windows that shine sunlight, a free anti-depressant, on my clients.

I can't write prescriptions from the oak office essentials placed at the back of the room since I'm not a psychiatrist, but I can write about who needs them. Repeatedly when delivery men don't watch where the hell they're sitting their deliveries down at. Now, I'm late for an appointment.

"T, deposit the flowers somewhere else like the trash," Paisley sounds off in my ear while I snatch two Kleenex tissues from the opened box on my desk.

"A normal girlfriend doesn't do that P, like I've been trying not to snoop through his belongings—"

"Normal girlfriends do that," she cuts in then giggles.

"But we both know I'm not a normal girlfriend anymore. He knows it too. I've turned down several, no *all* of his offers for dates. I don't get why he just doesn't give up. Well, actually I do get it. He's a nut."

"He may be a nut, but he's still a man. For them, it's one thing to get rid of a woman and another to lose her to someone one else. He's not stupid, T."

"Exactly, so why doesn't he just get rid of me then? I don't mind being broken up with." Well, until it's Robert doing the breaking up before we're even officially together.

And then the back of my eyes begins to burn.

Shit!

Paisley pays no attention to my sniffling since I'm already overdosing on pollen, as I try to get my emotions in check. It doesn't take me long, or for her to restart the chat between us.

"*You* wouldn't mind being broken up with, T. The rest of us do, especially when we're in love like Travis. He has to be if he wasn't cheating on you in the last two months when he was too busy to give you some. Men turn into minute men when they haven't been getting some, which means he was happy with you until he fucked up and let someone else in the picture that got some. Now, you have a stalker that lives with you that isn't getting some anymore. *Poor baby,*" she croons.

I don't know who she views as the poor baby, me or Travis.

"I have to go, P. No clients but I need to sign this paperwork and get to an appointment to view a condo today."

"So you're still moving out?"

"Yes. We're over. I'm done. Moving on." It's not a lie as long as I'm talking about Travis.

Robert's a much harder hill to hustle.

"What's the address? What about the baby? How are you going to handle that?"

"P, love, when someone says they have to go, you don't keep asking questions. You actually let them go because they might actually have something else to do, but I'll answer for you. The address is 1016 Mercer Boulevard—"

"Nice!"

It is nice, in a wealthy district that requires less wealth to move in than where I currently live, and it's on the north side of town, a whole section of town away from Travis. I can hear Paisley clicking away on her cell, reporting where I'm going to Robert's silent and unseen henchmen.

"Oh, and P, there's no baby until I find out differently in five more weeks at my check up, and I'll handle it by crossing one bridge at a time. I have to—"

"How are you going to keep Milani from ratting on you to her father if you're pregnant?"

"P, didn't I just explain what you're supposed to do when someone says they have to go?"

"Yep, but you didn't get it all the way out that time, so now you have to answer the question."

I sigh, now five minutes late for my appointment. I put her on speaker and send a quick text to my realtor to not leave. "I can't stop Milani from ratting on me, but I don't have to deal with her father until there's a DNA test done and then I won't have to deal with him then. He doesn't want any more kids." I realize I'm talking as if I'm indeed pregnant, which could easily lead to disappointment if I'm not.

"P, bye!" I swipe the end call button on my cell before she can get in one more question, and quickly sign the forms in front of me before grabbing my purse and high-tailing it out of the office door directly in front of me.

When I enter the waiting room that's dressed in tan carpet, matching walls, more fake floral arrangements, free standing racks full of magazines, and white-cushioned arm chairs, I drop the forms in the out box on my secretary's desk that sits left of my office door. Deidra Long waves me at without even looking up from her computer screen. For four years, she's been with me and as dependable as a twenty seven-year-old teen prostitute with three kids who wanted a better future for them all comes. That means she has lots of emergencies and needs to take half the morning or afternoon off to tend to them often, but that's life and I'm not one of those bosses that forget it.

She always makes up for it by coming in early and staying late to catch up on her work, and knows I won't be back today since I have no therapy appointments or work to catch up on myself. I can go home, and get that power nap, or snoop through Travis' things, but I have no worries that something will be left undone when I come back Monday morning. Deidra literally uses her work to get a break from her kids on the weekend, and I don't mind that either.

I push through the waiting room that leads to a long hallway covered in more tan carpet and walls and bigger fake floral arrangements. There's a crowd of people waiting at the elevator at the other end of the hallway. I decide it'll be easier and less crowded to just take the stairs, which open in a tiny alcove on the ground floor and is only a few more steps away from the front doors that open to the parking lot. Halfway down the staircase, I hear the stair's door open behind me, but the staircase turns, so I can't see who's coming down.

Probably just someone that didn't want to wait for the elevator too.

I develop as fast a pace as I can in black pumps, a fuchsia pink, sleeveless, and form-fitting dress with a high neck draped in a gold chain with a black teardrop diamond that sits between my free swinging breasts. They wouldn't be swinging at all if Paisley had let me get off the phone in time. Now, I'm late for a pit stop in the rest of my life, and push through the exit door for the stairs then cross the gray-tiled floor in the main lobby to the single glass door.

Two parking spots down, right in front of the exit, are where my gray Mercedes Benz sits. There's nothing spectacular about the car except the Benz symbol on the hood. I like understated but has a purpose, and that's to get me from point A to B. The alarm chirps when I point the key fob at the car, then heavy footsteps sound off the paved sidewalk behind me. I look back out of reflex. A heavily-built black man with a bald head above army fatigue pants, black combat boots, and a brown tee with the Army's logo on it is twenty feet back. It's not uncommon for soldiers who have been to war, needing someone's ear to bend about their experiences or just a checkup, to be in and out of this building where there are lots of medical offices.

I just don't like the hard stare in his eyes that he's directing my way as I open my driver's door and drop in my seat, while tossing my purse in the passenger's. He turns right on the sidewalk suddenly and hurries to a heavily-tinted black sedan four parking spots down from mine, like he's trying to keep up with me. The pit of my stomach hollows out. I don't know what I'm getting a bad omen about, but I don't dismiss it, and keep a close eye on the rearview mirror when I pull out of the parking lot. The black sedan finally enters the mirror, but he puts on his left blinker instead of his right, and actually turns that way. I exhale and slump in my seat while driving in the other direction to the north where the condo, a stepping stone to getting the hell out of Travis' life, waits for me.

Twenty minutes and the worst traffic jam known to man finally finds my rearview mirror too before I pull up at the gate for the winding complex that sits on several acres of land. A security guard steps out of a tiny booth between the entrance and exit lanes with a clipboard in hand, and leans down over me who's hanging out the driver's side window. When I show my ID and he confirms the realtor's waiting for me, he lets me through. I drive forward and grab the first visitor's parking spot I can find, which feels like its one mile away from every front door with a tiny walkway between patches of well-maintain lawns.

If the condo's owners are trying to discourage visitors, they're doing a remarkable job and I've already decided I don't want to live here. When Milani visits for the first time, she certainly won't come back after having to carry the baby and his needs on a hike in the heat just to see me, and I won't blame her for it. Still, I get out of my car anyway just to tell the realtor face to face to find a place that requires a less arduous and shorter journey to get to. Fortunately, the condos' front doors are on the ground level, so I don't have to climb anymore steps or find an elevator, but the raging sun beats down on my head as I make my way down the long sidewalk to the walkway for the condo I'm here to view.

My realtor, a gray-haired woman with streaks of black running through it with short stature and orthopedic shoes under a black skirt and red silk blouse, steps out the door of the condo just as I find the right address nailed to the side of the building. She tilts one side of her lips up, shakes her head, and holds up her hand. I stop walking, and wait for her to meet me at the end of the walkway. After she locks the door, she turns around, and a car drives past behind me. I glance back, recognizing the same black sedan that the ex-soldier climbed into. It creeps by. The pit of my stomach starts talking to me again, so does the realtor.

"Trinity, I'm so sorry, hun. I didn't know we had to be in top form to get to these apartments. This is my first time visiting them as well. I'll call you later with more options that I've at least visited once, if you're not throwing my old ass to the wind after this bullshit." I swear all the old people I know curse, and I would laugh too, but I'm too shook up from seeing the car that I thought I lost to react accordingly.

"It's okay, Mrs. Byrd. I'll be waiting for your call and I'm going now. Be safe."

I move between the parked cars, to at least try and get the tag number from the guy's car that's obviously following me.

"Is everything okay, Trinity?" Mrs. Byrd asks concerned from the end of the sidewalk as I step off.

I manage to get the last four digits of the license plate before the car speeds away. If there's only way in and out of the complex, there's every chance I'll be able to get the alphabets in front of the digits. All I have to do is wait for him to come out of the gate.

I wave back at Ms. Byrd and start my hike down the street to my car. Two sweaty armpits and a fuzzy head from the heat later, I jump inside my car, crank it, and snatch my phone from my bag on the seat. Paisley's office line rings twice before she answers.

"I think I might be having a long day after all, P, but I'm not sure yet, so wait for my text with some information that I want you to pass on to Robert before you send the other text to my rescuer. Whoever that may be for today," I say breathlessly as I back out and speed toward the exit side of the gate.

If I can beat the ex-soldier to the exit then reverse into a visitor's spot.

"What's going on, T? And don't be a hero," she hisses through the line, with anxiety riding her tone.

"I'm being followed. I just want to know who it is. I'm going to send you his tag number when I get it."

"No, Trinity. I'm going to send your rescuer to you. I don't think Robert has anyone following you."

"No, Paisley, don't. I just want to know who it is before we blow this operation to hell and back for no reason. It could actually be a guy that Robert sent. The dude wasn't trying to hide from me. Robert would be the only one that would allow his henchmen to be out in the open like that, right?"

"I don't know, T, and this is dangerous. You're out. This operation is over. Let the cops deal with Travis."

"P, just send Robert the tag number when I give it to you. If it's not his man, then I'm out."

"Okay, but that's how it's going down, or I'll come get your ass myself. I'm not losing you for some pharmacy pills that no one has the benefit of taking yet. I think I need something for anxiety right damn now. I wonder if there's a dealer on the corner of the business district these days."

I scoff, "Highly doubt that."

The soldier finally comes back down the other side of the road, driving slowly pass Mrs. Byrd, who's rambling around in the back seat of her tan Durango truck three spaces up from me. Then the black sedan screeches to a halt, as if he stomped on the brakes at the last second. His front end bouncing up and down confirms it.

My instincts scream for me to get the hell out of there. He starts backing up in a hurry. My nerves pull tight with tension. Sheen of sweat breaks out on my brow, even though I'm sitting in the midst of an arctic blast from my air conditioner.

"Shit, P! He knows I'm trying to get his tag and won't drive past me."

"Then *leave*, Trinity, and go home so someone can pick you up. I don't like this one bit."

"Me either, but we need to figure out who's man this is before I just ruin the operation, or we'll have done this all for nothing."

"Trinity! Damn near everything we do is all for nothing when we *all* die at some point and can't take anything we've worked for with us. You're not dying for a damn tag number, or I'll kill you myself. Now go home and get ready to go into hiding until this shit is over with or I'm going to lose my shit on you."

"Too late for that, baby—" The beep for an incoming text cuts me off. "Hold on, P."

"Trinity…" she starts to rant.

I take the phone from my ear, swipe the new text icon on my screen.

Ms. Regina Byrd-realtor

336-897-5632

FRG4567 Get his ass, Trinity.

I know immediately what she's done for me, then forward the text to Paisley, and respond back to Mrs. Byrd.

336-898-7954

That's the plan, Mrs. B. Thank you ❤

I shove the phone to my ear. "P, I got it or rather my realtor's got it.

It should be coming through your phone now."

"You haven't heard a damn thing I said have you?"

"No, and sorry, I was busy getting his ass. Now let me know what Robert says. I'm going home and I need to be alert."

"Don't think I don't know you're using me as a middleman between you and Robert."

It's true, and there's no point in lying to someone who already knows me frontwards and backwards.

"And I love you for it, P. Bye. Call me when you get the info." I hang up before she can call me out some more.

The drive home is a nerve wracking one. I spend more time looking in the rearview mirror for the black sedan than I do looking forward and speeding when I can get around traffic. My house doesn't come into view fast enough. I feel like it's much safer to be there with Travis, who may be there already, than in a car with no defensive-driving skills. He seems to be spending more time at home, harassing me about going on a date than tending to his pill-pushing business, and that's not good for the business I have going on behind his back. But I know what Travis wants from me. It's the ex-soldier's wants that concern me.

I reach up and press a button on the remote control for the garage that's clipped to my sun visor while scanning the street for the black sedan. The street is clear. Paisley has yet to call me back. I drive into the opened garage, parking beside Travis' navy-blue Ferrari parked there.

I'll got out only after the garage door has closed and Paisley has called. The garage is long, dark, and eerie, even during the daylight hours. If I sit out here today, I'll probably risk making Travis suspicious, but he's going to have to be suspicious. I need to prepare to deal with him, along with waiting for Paisley's call, and I'm not doing it in the dark, so I leave the garage door up. It would be easier for me if Paisley texted, but who's to say Travis isn't snooping through my things. Well, I can't say, and not taking any chances, including him overhearing my conversations.

As soon as I grip the phone tightly in one hand and erase Mrs. Byrd's text, an incoming call swamps the screen.

"P, what do you know?"

"This isn't Paisley, Trinity," a deep familiar voice replies, wraps around me like a warm casing while raising goose bumps on my arms.

My heart shudders in its fetal position in my stomach—it hasn't moved since I left Robert in his bedroom in Aruba.

"What are you doing at Paisley's job, Robert?" I ask breathlessly, as if I'm still taking that hike in front of the condo that I turned down.

"I'm not at her job," his voice comes through strong, which makes a shiver run down my spine and my head too heavy to hold up suddenly. "She's at my safe house three houses down from you on the other side of the street. You scared the shit out of her when you called."

I start to laugh—Paisley was running scared and ratting on me to Robert instead of doing as I asked her, but I already know good help's hard to find these days.

"Who's tail is he, Robert?" I want to get straight to the point then off the phone.

"Mine. Albert got made when you rushed out of the office. I'm sorry if he scared the shit out of *you*. He says you're too damn alert and smart by the way. Nobody has ever made him or tried to get his tag number before today, and he's pretty sure the realtor gave it to you."

Huge amounts of relief blossoms in my chest, and then it's gone. Robert still doesn't want me. I'm guess this is what Milani felt like when she discovered that he was having someone keep tabs on her, while he had no intentions of being in her life up close and personal like she needed him to be.

"Okay, Robert. Everything's fine and I'm going inside now. Don't send anyone to pick me up."

"How's the search for the condo going?" he asks suddenly.

"It's fine. Bye."

Small talk is not an option for us. It's torture listening to his voice. A knock on my window slings me out of my misery. I look up into Travis' frowning face. My nerves spring tight enough to be plucked.

Where did he come from?

I recall the side door off of the garage that opens into the back yard. He could've easily entered the garage from there, and I never saw him do it because I was too consumed with Robert's voice that was dulling my wits. Albert would be disappointed—I managed to catch him, and then I got caught.

I clutch at my heart and the phone, drop my head again, and swear that Travis has radar for when Robert and I are communicating. I press the control mechanism for the window with a shaking finger three seconds later.

When it's halfway down, I look up again. "Jesus Travis, are you *trying* to give me a heart attack?"

"Since when do you call Mr. Elliot by Robert, Trinity?"

Dammit! He was eavesdropping. Has to be Karma's ass making her rounds, and working on the wrong person.

"What?" I ask defensively, while trying to assemble my thoughts and lies. "Are we back on this again?"

When did *you start calling him Robert, Trinity?*

The moment I decided I wanted to be his and in his arms.

Now, you're in deep shit and more deep shit. How are you going to catch Travis in his if you're too busy getting caught in yours?

He crosses his arms that are draped in a white long-sleeve dress shirt above black slacks, and leans back on his car. "Yes we are."

I look out my front windshield. "Ah, I don't know, Travis. I guess during the baby shower when I saw how much he's changed. He's no longer the undercover criminal behind the businessman's disguise. He really does love Milani hard. I hope you can see why I identify with that, and it puts us on the same level somehow. Is that weird for you?"

What it is is an outright fib, and I'm getting good with coming up with them.

He exhales and looks down at his feet. "No, I guess not. Well, I have to go and tend to some—"

"Bank business," I cut in. "Go ahead. I'll chill at home for today, take a nap, and call up Paisley and maybe Milani too for a girl's night out *if* she's finally had the baby and can find a babysitter," I joke, and she's nowhere near having that baby though I've been through two fake false labor conversations since I got back. "You know how it is with babies. Well, actually you don't, but maybe you will one day."

I stop when I realize I'm rambling then ramble on some more. "Don't wait up if I'm not here when you get back."

I decide to just get out of the car to stop the rambling, and damn near hit him with the door while swinging it out. Almost step on his feet while getting out. He finally scrambles out of the way after giving me the once over when I stand up beside him, as if he's looking for something out of place, which he probably is, but all the messiness is on the inside. I rush to the door that leads into the sparsely decorated, long, and narrow kitchen with a few canisters shaped like magnolias and kitchen appliances on the marble countertop that stretches from the garage access I entered to the other end where the laundry room is.

The clicking of my heels on the large white tiles with a deep tan grout combined with Travis trailing me through the wide opening into the dining room grates on my nerves. I round the dining table and the chandelier that I was so proud of, moving for the wide opening on the other side of the room, which takes us into the living area. There's just a Victorian-era, cream colored, thick-cushioned loveseat and couch with regal pieces of cherry wood trim that encases and rises out the backs of the chairs, making them seem like thrones. Yes, Travis picked this furniture, and the only other furnishings in here with the chairs is a cherry wood table set that matches perfectly with the wood trimming of the furniture and cream lamps.

I realize I put more effort into decorating my office, then take a hard left toward the master bedroom where there's a little bit more furniture that suits my taste. Subconsciously, I knew I hadn't found the last home that I would live in and didn't waste much time decorating, but my bedroom has to be more than comfortable. I take my sex seriously, and this is where we spent most of our time anyway. Making love with Travis *was* the best part about him. I should've been getting to really know him, but the bedroom's the best place to avoid that because I never really wanted to know him. He served a purpose just as I did for him, and he took immense pleasure and his time in finding out what note my body would hum to.

"Don't you mean *we* will find out one day about kids, babe?" he asks from behind me.

"I... I don't think we ah..." I give up trying to explain just as fast as I started; shouldn't have ever said anything about babies in the first place and have now stuck most of my foot in my mouth.

I can't seem to find the right words to spit out around it either that would push him out the front door and back into the rocky zone that our relationship has resided in for two months. Hopefully, when I find the right words, they'll close the door that I just stupidly opened to our relationship issues too.

I take cover in the enormous square room of light-yellow walls with hanging knickknacks and large pictures framed with matching white and blue toile theme that the bed cover would be identical to if it didn't have yellow highlights throughout its design. I sling my purse and my tired ass down on the queen-sized pine bed before bowing my head. At this point, I just want some peace from Travis' pestering and the day that's gone absolutely horribly wrong. All I had to do was encounter the men in my life for that to happen, and that's just damn sad.

"You don't think what, Trinity?"

That I need to stay here any longer. You're rubbing off on me with the lying and bothering the hell out of me with the questions.

Now that I've thought about it, moving out would be a fabulous solution to stop him from pulling me into conversations I don't want to have, while he keeps track of me in the house, while Robert does the same thing outside of it.

"I'm thinking that maybe we need some space, Travis."

"Apart," he shrieks like a damn girl.

I doubt if Robert's throat is even capable of raising his voice that high.

There you go comparing the two.

I can't seem to help it either or thinking about how they're so different in bed. Robert more caring and Travis more demanding.

"Trinity!"

"What?" I snap back, and raise my head—a mistake since Travis is giving me the same look that Robert's operative was doing earlier.

"I'm fucking talking to you about our future and you're tuning me out."

Yeah. So? If only you knew what I was thinking about. Wait. Did he just curse me? Oh, he's pissed, huh?

I lift a finger in the air. "I'm going to be honest with you, Travis."

"Yes, please, and thank you," he replies mockingly.

I exhale, trying to keep from mimicking his behavior and turning this into a fight. "Look, we won't be finding out anything together in the future because we don't have one. I told you I'm not meant to be a permanent girlfriend, and I just don't see me as being more than that with you. It's time to cut our losses."

"Our losses?"

"Yes, our losses. I lose four years with the man I thought wanted to marry me, but that's better than losing forty years, and you can find the woman that doesn't mind playing second string to your bank business until a month away from it doesn't make you want to piss your pants." Never mind that you're a psychopath. "You can have anyone you want, and you know it, Travis.

"Piss my… *Trinity*, I'm not entertaining this shit today and you're not going anywhere. I want you and only you and I intend to *keep* you," he sneers at me.

CHAPTER 12

Who the hell is he talking to like that?

"Say what, Travis?"

"You fucking heard me. You're. Not. Going. Anywhere."

"Travis," I say quietly then cross my legs and knit my hands together slowly in my lap. "Have you been smoking meth? Or maybe it's me that's been smoking, because I could've sworn that you just told me, a grown woman by the way, that I'm. Not. Going. Anywhere."

He closes his eyes. "I haven't smoked anything. You better not. And that's *exactly* what I said." The real Travis, domineering and controlling, emerges finally, but he should go back to wherever he came from because he has the wrong black woman today.

"No you didn't say that, Travis," I reply calmly.

"Yes the hell I did."

"No… you *didn't.*"

I rise from the bed to the closet that's almost directly on the other side of the room, where a gift from Milani and Paisley for my twenty-first birthday waits for me to pack it with all the belongings that I can fit in it. The Louis Vuitton suitcase loiters besides the one from Aruba that I haven't unpacked. Yeah, I should just grab that suitcase and go.

"Damn it, Trinity, wait!" he yells.

I stop on the dime, completely taken aback by the violence in his tone, peering back him with wide eyes. He starts to run his hand through his hair, angling his head toward the floor, a sign of him bowing down. Thank God.

"I don't want you to go anywhere, Trinity. Does that sound better? And I'm sorry if I'm too aggressive right now. Business isn't going how I wanted it to. I don't want to lose you, and it's all running together and badly, making me crazy. I didn't mean to take it out on you. I'm sorry."

I swallow loudly, and don't believe a word he's saying. "Your apology doesn't change anything, Travis. We're going nowhere, and you need to get use to that. I can stay here till the cows come home and you can send me all the flowers from every florist in the state. We're still not going to be together."

I could tell him that his side business of pushing pills isn't going well because Robert's calling the shots now, but I won't.

His face transforms to a mask of pure fury. "*Is that why you were at Sunset Townhouses on Mercer today?*" he screams like a raving lunatic, which he is now, that's keeping outside tabs on me too.

"Yes. I haven't found a place suitable for me to move into yet but I can stay at a hotel until I do because what you won't be doing is screaming at me like a petulant child that just had his toys taken away. How do you know where I was anyway?"

He rushes across the room toward me. I turn around to face him so he doesn't have a chance to take me from the blind side, completely paranoid at this point. He stops right in front me. I drop my right foot back and ball my hands into fists. I know how much damage I can do to him and where all of his weak spots are. If he reaches for me in anyway, he'll find out where his weak spots are too.

"I tracked your cell phone, but that doesn't matter. Just give me a chance to make things right between us," he growls from his height that makes him almost a full head taller than me and very intimidating.

"Oh Travis, it matters and regardless of what your crooked ass mind tells you, I have the right to call the end to our relationship as well as you do. Why don't you do it already and put us both out of our misery? You obviously don't trust me."

That makes for a bad relationship with narcissists *and* non-narcissists.

"And for good reason, Trinity, I don't trust you anymore because you won't let me be the man I used to be, by letting me love you in all the ways I know makes you happy," he snarls.

"And I'm miserable, don't trust you, and that's why I'm looking for another place to live," I fire back, then watch all the fury in his face fades away as his rigid stare fills with realization that we aren't going backwards to how things used to be.

"You really mean that, don't you?" he asks with awe maligning the low pitch of his voice.

I nod then stand tall again. He seems to be coming around to my way of thinking. His mouth begins to open and close like a fish, and then he starts to turn in half circles. Well, that's not good.

When he finally returns his gaze to me, there's more desperation in his eyes than I've ever seen anyone exhibit before now. Loss of control must be a new thing for him.

"Okay, Trinity. You can stay here. I'll move—"

"No, Travis," I interrupt.

If I staying here, it's just another form of control for him. He can monitor everything I do without even being here and have free access to me while keeping me isolated. Abusive people work that angle first once they start to seek complete control of their victims. "Your father brought this house. It's not fair to you if I stay, so I'll go and—"

"What's the difference between Robert and me besides eighteen years, Trinity? I'll tell you. I'm a boss. He *used* to be a boss. Shit, I'm an upgrade compared to his has-been ass. Does he even know the difference between a psychologist and a psychiatrist?"

"Does it matter?"

"Humor me," he spews into the air, infecting me with his anger.

"Fine! You asked for it, Travis. Robert hasn't asked me to marry him only to change his mind later, embarrassing the hell out of us both.

You're a deceptive little shit only concerned with being more powerful than your father. Well, you can stop comparing yourself to him too. You'll just a brat in a suit that thinks he has something to prove. Well, go prove it Travis, and leave me the hell alone."

I start to spend in circles this time, then twirl back to him, with my pointer finger raised in the air, succumbing to my anger and descending into full rant mode. "And another thing, there *is* no other man and the other difference between you two is Robert's too old to play games with his relationships and worry about supposed threats to them. You're still wet behind the ears in that department if you think there's anything going on with me and him. This is why I'm leaving. I need a man that hasn't been chasing Robert's *has-been* ass since we met. And do *you* even know the difference between what I do and a similar field?"

His eyes narrow on me, and I recognize when I inserted my other foot in my mouth. Should've kept calm and quiet.

"How do you know that, Trinity?"

"How do I know what, Travis?" I ask innocently.

"That I've been chasing Robert, *Trinity*," he spits my name out like it's poison.

"I have eyes and I'm a psychologist." More like ears and I'm an eavesdropper.

If I don't shut up, he'll know that too.

"You haven't seen me act odd around Robert, and I sure as hell never asked you to set up a meeting with him for me because you would've nagged until I told you why I wanted it. I didn't want you screaming at me about doing the wrong thing and trying to talk me out of it. I don't *want* to be talked out of it, so how do you know, Trinity?"

I wonder when he got to know me better than I know him and why I let that happen. Now, I need a way to throw him off the same trail that Robert and I didn't want him on.

"You don't know what I've seen or heard since these are my eyes and ears, now do you? Want to tell me what it is that you wanted from Robert anyway? You were real eager to get to Aruba and no man wants to go to a baby shower that badly. You practically beat everyone on and off the plane getting there." Then I narrow my eyes and step closer to him. "Or is it Milani that you wanted to see so badly? You two have never liked each other, but there's a thin line between love and hate and it's easy to cross over. I can take the truth, Travis. Is it my best friend that you want to be with now?"

Milani's going to kill me when I tell her that I've thrown her under the bus and rolled over her too, to save my own skin and the investigation.

Travis frowns like someone fed him sour grapes then leans back from me as I'm waving a hissing cobra in his face. "What? Milani? Half of Miami has run through her and you think *I* want her?"

"First of all, no one talks about my girl like that but me, and even I don't do it in that way, so you can stop doing it and don't *ever* do it again. Second, people tend to demean others as a defensive reflex when they've been caught up in feeling some type of way for a person they shouldn't be feeling anything for, and third—"

"There's only one way to stop you from thinking that about me and Milani," he cuts me off with a wide grin on his face suddenly, his mood changing like the wind.

"What way is that?" I snipe, praying he doesn't say 'marry me', but at least I'm not having to accuse him of Milani anymore.

"Let's go to Vegas," he blurts out—not saying what I thought he would, but he's about to, and I should nip that in the bud.

"No."

"Yes. You know you want to elope with me. Forget about the caterers and venue. Let's do it fast and spend the whole weekend there with no working phones or internet, just you and me."

I harrumph, ejecting hot air in his face. "You've lost your mind if you think I'm settling for a quickie wedding and honeymoon. I want the real thing or nothing."

Hard evidence of his illegal activities and him behind bars is more preferable, and he can think I'm a gold digger all he wants to in the meantime.

He reverts back to raging mad. "You don't want *me*, but there's no other man? Is that what you're saying, Trinity? Because I don't fucking believe it. You're just trading one kingpin for another, so what makes you think you've upgraded?"

Maybe he doesn't realize that he just called himself a kingpin, but I sure as hell did. If he's forgetting to keep his secret covered, he's beyond caring if I know what he's been up to, and I'm in danger.

"Travis," I say calmly then walk closer to him, intending to soothe him in any way I have to. "There's no other man, especially not Robert. I don't know why you're so stuck on that." I get two steps within his personal space, thinking I'm making an impact on his mood. "If there was, I would tell—"

Travis' hands strike out like lightning before I can finish. His fingers are biting into my shoulders as if they're snakes who are hanging on to me by their fangs before I can blink. I'm being shaken like a rag doll before I can regain my defensive position and find his weak spots. Nelly and Tim McGraw begin to croon Over and Over Again off in the distance before I can think of a way to defend myself, after letting Travis lull me into a false sense of security with his moving out suggestion.

"Do you think I'm fucking stupid, Trinity?" he shouts in my face, while making my brain bounce off my skull and my neck snap back and forth.

I use what scrap of alertness I have left and grab onto the lifeline of the ringing phone that could be an important phone call about his side business. "Travis, stop! Your phone! Your…"

I trail off when I feel myself sinking to my knees, can't hold my own weight up anymore, with the wind knocked out of me. All my senses cower in the far corner of the room.

When I open my eyes, Travis is standing over me. I wouldn't even know that if his feet covered in expensive dress shoes that I bought him weren't in my fuzzy line of vision. He delivers a breathless hello into his phone. I'm not sure at what point I closed my eyes, but I realize right away that it was stupid to come back here with Travis. He's pinned me in a corner.

"That's good to hear, Robert," Travis says happily. "I've been waiting for that news all week."

I look down at the navy-blue carpet beneath me and think, *Well, at least one of us got what they wanted. He's about to rise to the biggest pill pusher in Miami and they'll be lowering my ass in a casket if I don't get out of here.*

But I have no way of alerting Robert that Operation Disturbing has took a turn for explosive or that Travis has escalated to full-on abuser. How did I get here?

I'll tell you how; by a stupid sense of self-confidence that led me to believe that I could one up Travis then take him down. I'll probably die for that mistake. I'm not going to make it easy for him to kill me though by just kneeling here. I lift one knee then plant a foot on the floor.

Travis' foot lifts off. The bottom of his shoe makes contact with my raised knee, and then he pushes. I tumble backwards. My hands automatically drop palms down to break my fall, but they crumple and I land on my ass and elbows.

Not one to give up, I brace my forearms on the floor and attempt to push off then get up, but I can barely hold up my head, which feels like it's made of helium. It bobs backward between my shoulder blades as if it's not fastened down properly on my neck—Travis literally shook the firing ability out of the neurons that send messages through my brain, causing my fine-motor skills to be nonexistent.

I'm not going to be able to sit up let alone get up any time soon, but

I can't just lay here with just Travis in the room either. The urge to scream wells up inside of me. "Robert!"

Yes, most people would've yell help, but at some point, he became my savior. I'm praying that he's up for the job and still only three houses away because his number is up.

Travis exhales into the phone. "I was so hoping she wasn't going to do that, but I should've known better."

"We both should have," I comment with a slur like I've drunk one too many.

The drunkenness will go away when my brain reconnects the severed neurological links, and that's going to take some time. Then the world goes black, until I start to dream about Robert. He's standing over me, commanding me to wake up while tapping gently on my right cheek. I open my eyes anyway. Then I have to wait for them to focus, on the two Travis' who are leaning over me in a room much, much darker than it was before. The sliver of a quarter moon shines through the open panels of the curtains on the opposite wall several feet away from the foot of the bed. I don't need much light to tell when the twins smile down at me, can feel the evilness rippling off them.

"Finally, I thought you were going to be out all night," they say together.

My throat works to swallow the sudden dryness in it. "Travis—"

"Don't start, Trinity."

Both Travis' walk away from the side of the bed. In their trek toward the eight-drawer dresser with a majestically-designed hand carved top piece that would touch a low ceiling, the twins meld into one psycho. That's good for me mentally, still not so good physically since Travis is physically attacking me now, but at least I'm not all shook up anymore.

Travis opens the top drawer and extracts a silver object with a grip and muzzle.

When in the hell did he get a gun?

It shouldn't be possible for more fear to pack itself inside my body, but it does and sends me to a sitting-up position. It's amazingly much easier to get up now than the last time I tried. I slide to the edge of the bed. I'm shocked he picked me up off of the floor at all now that he's escalated. All humanity is gone from the abuser and victim at this point—one throws theirs away, the other is stripped of it.

Since I like my humanity just the way it is and where it is, I decide it's time to play nice, like *really* nice with Travis even while his back is turned. I have no weapon of my own to take advantage of his position.

"Travis, there's no need for the gun. Just tell me what you want from me."

He holds the weapon up then brandishes it by twisting it from side to side as if he's inspecting it, which is giving me major heart palpitations.

"It's too late for that, Trinity" he says softly, an ear-piercing warning that the situation had gone from explosive to hitting its flash point. "How much do you know about my business?"

"I know nothing about being a vice president."

He twists around slowly until he's facing me with a look cold
enough to refreeze Alaska. "You're lying, Trinity. I know you overheard
my conversation on the phone in Aruba. You've been acting strange
every since. I know you want Robert too, because you haven't wanted
me to touch you since you started acting strange around him. I even
know that you love him, because you've called out his name every single
night in your sleep since we've been back, but I still love your trifling ass
and want you by my side when I take Miami. I've forgiven you for
wanting someone else. I just need you to be *my* girl again. Do you
understand me?"

The blood in my veins ices over and severe panic makes me fidget
on the bed. My eyes shift to the opened doorway beside him, but running
for the door with a small view into the dining room and making me a
moving target for the gun isn't even an option. I raise one hand. T

"Travis—"

"Lies!" he hurls at the top of his lungs.

I flinch, and throw both hands.

He closes his eyes and bows his head before stroking his temple
with the muzzle of the gun then starts to take deep breaths like he's
desperate to calm down. "Everything out of your mouth will be lies, until
you tell me the truth. We'll stay right here in this room until I think
you've told me the truth and I've convinced you that it's in your best
interest to be mine, again."

I say nothing, or everything that comes out my mouth will be just what he thinks it is; lies. The truth will set him off for sure, digging my grave faster.

"Do we have an understanding, Trinity?"

I nod viciously. A shadow emerges in the corner of the dining room wall that's in my limited view from the bed. I want to shout help at whoever's trying to rescue me out of a situation that I caused by simply wanting to know something that I'm no closer to getting the hard evidence for than the day I overheard his phone call. But if I don't put him away for life, he'll never stop coming after me.

"Travis," I call out.

The shadow freezes on the wall then vanishes. Travis opens his eyes. I shudder under his dead stare. If there's such a thing as miracles, I can get Travis to confess to his side dealings and whoever's just entered the house will have some sort of recording device on them. If they don't, having an upstanding connection with the police that'll take whoever's in the dining room at their word is good too, like the rapport an undercover officer would have, which I'm starting to think Robert is. Bob the Builder just an image that he'll do *anything* to keep. That makes his legal businesses the real front for what he really does for the law that'll do anything to get its man, including turning one into a criminal to catch another.

Here goes everything.

"Travis, suppose I stay with you. I—"

"Oh you're staying, no doubt about that. And Robert better think twice before trying to take you away from me. He's been calling me, checking on you since you passed out."

A device slides along the floor around the corner of the wall that separates the living room from the dining room. Please let it have one hell of a recording range. "I'm assuming that you want me to run Miami with you, but I only know bits and pieces about how you're going to do that from the conversation that I did hear in Aruba. How does a psychologist fit into your plans?"

He smiles widely. "As the woman I love, silly. I have a genius plan that's set in motion now thanks to Robert. You should know he offered me whatever I wanted for a little of nothing just to make sure you're still breathing."

"So you used me to make Robert bend and what's so genius about your plan?"

He places his back against the chest of drawers. "I didn't have to use you. He offered me a deal when he heard you scream his name, and there are no other dealers in pharmaceutical narcotics. It's too risky to deal pills since they're heavily government-regulated, but the risk is worth it if you're willing to take it, and I am. I won't just make a shit ton of money since there are no heavyweight competitors, I'll make *all* the money. My pop's banks will look like toys compared to my businesses, and nothing illegal will lead back to us. I have a crew to do the dirty work of collecting the product from every pharmacy that I can flip right here in Miami, so no middleman fees for importing the product from out of state and no security checks on land or water to worry about on my end thanks to Roberts. I'm even opening my own bank, shell companies, and check cashing places to launder the money. I still think I need my father's banks though and I intend to get them because there's going to be truckloads of money to be made off my monopoly." Then he looks down at the floor. "You know, Trinity, I was doing business at night with contractors, designers, and my crew. I never cheated on you with anyone."

Too bad I can't say the same.

I tilt my head to the side, as if this conversation is getting titillating by the second, and it is. "Who are your crew and the people that'll hurt you all if you don't pay them on time?"

His eye narrow on me. "Why are you asking all these questions now? You could've asked me about everything since Aruba."

"Because before now, I didn't want to know. Just wanted out of what you had gotten yourself into. It didn't sound safe for me, even less for you when you were talking on the phone. But if I'm going to be a part of this, I need to know what I'm getting myself into like any good businesswoman would do."

He tilts his lips up at one side and cocks his head in understanding. "Makes sense. My crew is Blair Costo, Owen Hardy, and Shane Murray. You'll meet them later tonight. They're nice guys that are a bit skittish and used to work for my father's bank in Tallahassee. They're not really cut out to be gangsters either but they're loyal, college-educated, and tired of the rat race. They all want the same thing, money, and lots of it. I just want to give you the world, Trinity."

"What about the men who'll hurt you all? Are they dangerous enough to hurt me too?"

"I had to borrow my start up cash for my empire from loan sharks in the Mezzane Cartel out of Cuba. I could buy the pills myself, but you know the first rule of business. Never—"

"Use your own money," I finish for him.

"The Mezzane crew is dangerous, sleazy ass guys, but a necessary evil," he says distastefully then screws up his mouth like he really does have a bad taste in it. "One of their soldiers came into the bank a year before I met you, to set up a fake business account for a shell company so he could launder the money the cartel makes in Miami. He looked out of place in the teller line even in a business suit, like you did, and I pulled him into my office too because I wanted to know what dirty shit was he into. I let it slip that I could launder his money in a much faster way for a price. I'm the VP of the bank. Who would question what I do there?" This would be the first time he'd gotten into bed with criminals.

"But you knew who I was when you pulled me out of line, didn't you?" I ask quietly, ashamed that I'd allowed myself to be scammed by him, but I want him to admit it.

He sighs, then strokes his brow with the muzzle of the gun again. "Unfortunately, I did, Trinity. The chance meeting with the soldier just pushed me over the edge. His suit was more expensive than mine, and I'd been just considering getting into the shadier side of business before that. I decided it was time to stop living in my father's shadow and eating from his table. He and the cartel were doing good business in Miami, but the biggest boss here was Bob. He's worth hundreds of millions of dollars cash money, without adding the wealth of his investments, so I had a background check run on him, looking for his closest connections a few months after I met the Mezzane soldier. But I can do better than Robert, Trinity. *I* can give you more."

At the moment, Travis is giving me acute indigestion—he'd targeted all of us, not just me if he was looking for connections to Robert.

"So that's why you asked me out, to get to him?"

He nods reluctantly. "At first, I approached Milani, but she wasn't into me even a little bit. I waited a few months and for her to forget about me coming on to her at Paradise Lounge before I approached Paisley, who was a little bit more difficult to get to." Then he smiles the grin of the victorious. "Her parents were throwing her a twenty-first birthday party at The Bellevue."

I was there at the restaurant only affordable to the rich and damn near famous if you're not already. "I didn't see you there that night, and it was invitation only."

"Well, I was. All I had to do was bribe the hostess, and I was in. Paisley's parents had her surrounded and on a pedestal like she was the best thing since sliced bread, but I overheard some guys talking about her parents having any guy that wanted to date her investigated before you could smell her breath. I couldn't risk them looking too deeply into me and finding my Mezzane connection, but I was reluctant to approach you. You were too beautiful and too intense. I knew I'd get distracted from my game, but by then, I was desperate to get the ball rolling and suddenly you were there at the bank like an oasis. I took my first drink of you, and my pops started asking questions about my decisions at the bank, like your startup money for insistence. You should've only gotten a third of what I approved you for, since most businesses fail in the first year, but I knew you'd succeed. You have that air about you that just breeds money and hard work even though you come for nothing. My connections with the Mezzane's heads got tighter once they offered to loan me money. Then I ran across Shane, Owen, and Blair in the break room at the Tallahassee bank location, talking about starting their own businesses in whatever made the most money. I think they were joking, but I approached them anyway. They've been on board ever since. Things just started to fall into place once I started to date you. You became my lucky charm."

I snort. "And I was hoping your family's success would rub off on me." Too bad it's not enough for him.

"We rubbed off on each other, Trinity."

"Do you have suppliers lined up now?"

"That's what Robert was for, to put me in touch with a major supplier. I was going to start out small with the pharmacies, but you have to grow or be absorbed by bigger thinkers. Blair will pick up our first major shipment through Robert's channel tonight at the Maritime Harbor on Sussex Beach. It took him a week to set it up, which is why I was so damn irritable when you got here. I thought he had more clout and could work magic, but it's done now. I don't ever have to crunch numbers again for a measly $250,000 a year or worry about what suppliers I'll miss making contact with, while spending a month long honeymoon with you. My goals would've been met sooner if I hadn't gotten distracted by you after our first kiss on the second date. Four years flew by. No time at all for a man in love."

"Then why did you call off the wedding?"

"Because I hadn't made nearly enough money that you deserve yet. This is all for you, Trinity."

Now, I want to scream at him, "Lies!" This ball was rolling before I entered the picture.

"Travis, I didn't need a bunch of money, just a real wedding and your child would've been enough for me."

Black rage fills his face. "Not for me, Trinity!" he shouts as expected.

Still, I cringe, then wait for him to continue.

"If you want a damn island, I want to be able to buy it, and my father thinks the way he runs his banks is what sets him apart from everyone else! I don't know why! He lets the bankrupt go without paying him for months, and the rich too, if they have a good enough sob story! It's the amount of money in your account, not the bank it's in that sets you apart! That's why he won't have his banks for much longer!"

"Travis, it what's in your heart that makes you the richest or poorest man on earth. You had it all, but you're letting your greed get in the way. Your father runs his business the way he does because he gets to help people like me who came from nothing but will work hard, and I only needed a third of the money you gave me. The rest just sits in the bank, collecting dust while I'm miserable because I lost everything when you called off the wedding; the only thing I really wanted from you."

"You didn't lose anything, Trinity! I'm still here!" He beats his chest with a closed fist, not really listening to what I said.

I never wanted him, just the image that came with him; successful, driven, and far away from the east side, and I'm not going to tell him that's what I meant either.

"The Travis I dated is gone. He didn't hurt or neglect me to make money he hasn't made or threaten to ruin small business owners so they'd supply him with a product for his own cartel."

He commences to beating his chest and shouting again. "And maybe the Travis you dated didn't launder money for the cartel through Diamond's either, or have Owen hiring a hit man to track my father home and kill him! And maybe the Travis you dated isn't planning to kill Robert as soon as Blair calls and says he's picked up the first of regular shipments at the harbor. That Travis you dated was a chomp living in his father's shadow, but the Travis standing before you isn't, and you're stuck with him!"

More than me and the ones I love are in danger, so is Travis' loved one. How trifling does Travis have to get before he realizes that he's gone too far?

If he hasn't given enough hard evidence for the recorder lying on the floor in the next room, he won't, because I've been in this corner long enough. Operation Disturbing is over.

CHAPTER 13

"Well that's enough talking for now. I'm hungry. Let's go out to eat," I say nonchalantly.

"Wait, Trinity, one more thing. Are you pregnant?"

"No," I answer quickly, maybe too quickly.

Travis scowls then charges across the room toward me. I have enough time to plant my hands on the bed then push myself further back on it, away from him and the gun that's pointed directly at me, before he reaches out and grabs a fistful of my hair then sinks down on the bed beside me. He sticks the business end of his weapon under my chin. At this point, I wish I had just run for the door, and took a chance of being shot than having him this close to me. At least I'd be closer to my rescuer.

"You're lying, Trinity!"

I reach for his forearm with the gun and his chest then push. "I'm not!"

He pulls me with him, embedding the muzzle deeper into the underside of my face. "Stop struggling, and tell the damn truth! You're not taking the damn birth control anymore!"

The only way he'd know that is if he's been counting them. I'll bet my life that he has, and hasn't just been keeping tabs on me since we got home but for the entire four years we've been together. I had better tell the truth.

"I don't know right now okay! I still have the birth control pills in my system but I missed one the same day we had sex in Aruba. If I am pregnant, I don't want to hurt the baby with the hormones in the pills."

I stare up at Travis through a coat of tears. Feels like he's ripping my hair out of the root. I so wish I wore weave with clips right now, because I'd rip the clips out myself, leave the weave in his hand, and make tracks for the door. I'm going to have to talk him down.

"How do you know I'm not taking them?"

Suddenly, he jerks away and bounces off the bed, returning to his spot by the chest. Massive amounts of relief pour through me and my scalp.

He starts to bump the weapon across his cranium and pace. "I count them every day, just like I keep track of your cycle. You can't have a baby right now, and nothing else will happen in this family that I don't want to. I didn't say anything about it when we came back from Aruba because we were already rocky and that's my fault for letting you think I hadn't been satisfying you."

What the hell does he mean by letting me think it?

212

He stops pacing to look directly at me. "Robert satisfied you while we were in Aruba though, didn't he? Don't lie to me because after you went to sleep, I checked your panties. They were wet. Once you're heated up, you have to have sex or it drives you crazy. I know you, Trinity. Your body takes over when you're aroused and you have fucked my brains out too many times to count in your sleep. Those two months you thought you weren't getting laid, you were and you didn't even know it, but I thought you were satisfied. You're like a fucking sex goddess and machine and don't even …" Travis voice fades out as I sink into severe shock—I've been molesting the man in my sleep.

Am I that different from normal women when it comes to my body sexually? What would've happened if I had stayed with Robert in Aruba?

For a woman who prides herself on her behavior when she's awake, you don't have a leg to stand on when you're not. Now that's trifling, Trinity!

"Shit! I'm sorry, Travis," I whisper then realize he's still rambling.

He throws his head back, and starts to laugh maniacally. "For what, Trinity? Being every heterosexual man's dream woman?"

Well, I guess Travis doesn't mind me attacking him at night, but there's one man whose dream woman I'm not, and he's the only one that I want to be that for.

Travis stops to peer right through me. "I can't let you go, Trinity. You're everything. Wife material. You'll be a good mother, but not yet. You take care of home. I haven't wanted for anything since we met. I know what I have in you, and I need it like the air I breathe."

Now, he's executing complete control over me. If I stay here with him, he'll have it because he'll take it. I jump to my feet, just as someone rushes around the corner of the dining room dressed in all black, almost blending in with the darkness in the house, barreling my way. Travis pivots toward the approaching figure as soon it steps over the threshold of the bedroom.

"He has a gun!"

Travis points his at the man with broad shoulders and taller than the average man. My stomach, with my heart still in it, bottoms out. I realize it's Robert. The last thing I want is him anywhere near Travis, but he's already pointing a gun at Travis' head from the bedroom's doorway, as I stand frozen with paralyzing terror coursing through my veins.

"Put the gun down, Travis." Robert's order is muffled by a ski mask covering his head. "The only air you'll breathe from now on will be regulated by the government just like those pills you're waiting on that aren't coming. But your boys are going down right along with you, so you're not the only one that'll be sucking on can-cooled air in prison, among other things."

"Not in this lifetime," Travis growls, before the sound of a rocket blasting off in close quarters permeates the room.

A flash from the business end of Travis' muzzle lights up the darkness long enough for me to see Robert get blown back two feet before he hits the floor on his back. He lays there sprawled out while someone suddenly starts screaming bloody damn murder. I don't know who the chick is that's screaming. Personally, I prefer to crawl inside myself, but my feet do their own thing and propel me forward. Not towards Robert's body either.

Even though in my rational mind I know he's dead after taking a bullet point blank to the chest or at least needs immediate help, primal law demands justice for Robert's senseless death and the right annihilate any threats to my unborn that I may or may not carry. I'd like to live too, so my feet direct me towards the killer who's still standing.

Travis raises his head to look sideways at me frenziedly, like a man who's understanding that he's just taken a life. I rush his profile lit up by two thick beams of moonlight reflecting off his white shirt. We collide with the chest of drawers beside him. He takes the brunt of the impact with his shoulder, and lets out a loud oomph before something lands on my foot. I suspect it's the gun, and then lose the rest of my mind by stepping back to punch and kick with the wild abandon of a woman that has nothing to lose and everything to live for.

After he takes my right fist to the nose, he reaches up to cover it with both hands. My fists keep raining blows as fast and as hard as I can deliver them. I pummel his raised hands, trying to get to his nose again.

He starts blocking my shots with his forearms while giving me a look lethal enough to frighten a small animal to death. "You bitch!"

I step back with one bare foot, draw my fist back, and punch him in the abdomen. He bends over predictably, to protect his middle while he keeps his damaged nose sheltered. I thrust a knee up into his forehead and watch his head snap back before I drive an elbow into his spine and him downward to his knees on the floor where the gun lies, which he reaches for. I kick at him. He swats my foot away, throwing me off center. When I catch my balance, then whirl back around, he's already standing up and pointing the gun at me.

"Hit me again bitch, and I *will* kill you," he sneers nasally.

I believe him, so I stand still but in the defensive position, more than ready to hit him again if he takes his eyes off of me long enough. Then Robert sucks up all the air in the room in one breath below me, coughs, and then wheeze. I glimpse down, relieved to hear some sign of life still left in him. A blow lands on my shoulder and pushes.

Suddenly, I'm lying on my back beside Robert. Impulse drives me to flip over his body then lay on top of him, refusing to leave him as an easy target for anymore bullets. Travis is going to kill me anyway, and it's my fault that he's in all of our lives. It's now my responsibility to give Robert a fighting chance to live because Milani and Jaden need him. Milani will certainly kill me anyway, if Robert dies and Travis doesn't get to me first.

"So that's where you want to be, Trinity, huh?" Travis asks. "You should've told me you prefer to be on the floor with the criminals and animals. Now you can die with them."

I close my eyes then bury my head between Robert's face and his shoulder, wishing I could feel the warmth of his skin on mine through the thin layer of the mask. Instead, I cup my hand over his forehead, and wait for death to be delivered to me from the next bullet that launches out of Travis' hand, while praying Robert's men will rush in and save him at least.

His hands glide up my back then stop when his arm is laying along the length of my spine and back of my head, as if he's trying to protect the vital parts of my body too even while he's dying. Then he squeezes me tightly. At least I'll die in his arms, where I've wanted to be since I left Aruba, but not for this reason.

"I'm sorry, Robert. I didn't know he was trying to get to you through me. You can't die... not like this," I whisper.

"Shhh, sweetheart, I can't hear," he whispers back fiercely before the expected gunshot goes off above me.

Before I can ask what is he listening for, glass shatters somewhere in the house and I wince then wait for the pain to begin somewhere in my backside before death ends it all. Seconds pass before something hits the ground in the same area that Travis is standing in, but no pain comes to me. Or it's just a miracle that I haven't felt it yet.

God, if you're listening, I need a miracle for Robert too.

A door slams somewhere in the house. Someone rushes into the bedroom on what seems like heavy large feet that go pass then come back and stop beside our heads. A presence looms over our bodies like a thick fog settling over us. I begin to shake. Unholy fear drips into my system like a slow acting poison. It could just as easily be one of Travis' men coming to finish the job he started with killing us.

"Bob, you and Trinity can quit playing possum now," Rhys jokes. "Travis is down from a sniper shot to the back of his dome. Won't be selling anything but passes to get in the pearly gates of hell. Good plan by the way, Bob. Let's do this again, but not anytime soon." And then,

Rhys is gone along with his big presence and fucked up sense of humor.

Milani warned me it's horrible during the worst times. Well, even the best of men has flaws.

I gasp, taking my turn at sucking up all the air in the room, wanting to believe that it's finally over, but that won't happen until I see the whites of Robert's eyes and he tells me for himself that he's okay. I lift my head up. His hand slips away then reaches under his chin and raises the ski mask that fits like a second skin over his face. When he opens his eyes, I scream. I don't know why, but that's what I do.

"Sweetheart, we're okay!" he yells back.

I stop losing my shit, suddenly completely exhausted. "I... I think I need we both need an ambulance, Robert."

Robert's eyes dilate, then he flips me over onto my back. "Were you shot?" he asks, frantic.

I stare up at the ceiling. Someone turned on the light. "I... I don't know but you were shot. I just needed to make sure he didn't do it again. You can't die. Milani would kill me."

Robert kneels over me, examines the front of my body with his eyes before placing his hands under my body and rolling me over. "I'm fine, sweetheart, but you..."

At this point, I'm not hearing anything he's saying, because I'm talking too with no idea of what I'm saying either, but I do know that I'm cold suddenly.

"Dammit, Trinity! We need a bus! She's going into the shock!"

I manage to form one coherent thought inside my head that's growing fuzzier by the second. "Don't cops say bus for ambulances?"

Robert rolls me back over then plops down on his ass beside me before pulling me into his arms, across his lap. "Sweetheart, listen to me. Travis didn't shoot you or hurt me. We shot him."

Then he starts to rock with my face buried in his neck. I remember nothing after that—I guess I'd heard all I needed to hear and was where I should've been since the day Robert told me to use his first name. I'm safe in his arms now, so I pass the hell out again.

*** Sixteen hours later ***

For six hours now, I've been staring at the ceiling and listening to the rhythmic beeps of hospital machines that are keeping really noisy records of my vital signs while I wait to be discharged. The ER doctor has already come and gone, after bringing me x-rays of my head and spine then ordering me to rest since I'll be here for another eight hours of observation.

"What else do you have to do, Ms. Moody?" he asks.

'Move the hell out of Miami' comes quickly to mind. Except, thanks to Travis' cock strong puny ass, I also have to wear a neck brace and suffer from whiplash for a week or two. At least there's no brain damage from being shaken like an adult baby. Hopefully, my blood pressure, which dropped too low by shock after Robert was shot, will keep rising so I can leave the hospital. While I'm here, I get to think about how I'm an official victim of domestic abuse, one who's unable to thank their savior.

I haven't seen Robert since he held me after the shit storm in my bedroom. The first thing I did when I woke up here is ask Paisley where is his room. She told me he doesn't have one. Didn't need one. He had on a bulletproof vest. So he didn't need that last miracle that I asked God for either. However, I need it, to do something about this empty space in my chest. Unless my savior saves me again, the void's probably going to stay for a while. I should probably just get used to it if I want to keep my right mind and dry eyes.

Paisley, who has stuck by my bedside along with Tasha and Frederick Booker gone to get their fourth cup of coffee, has been filling me in on what happened after I passed out for the second time in one day. Unfortunately for Paisley, I do more self-evaluating than listening when she talks. I seem to have no interest in knowing what happened after I blacked out. Wanting to know things put me in the hospital and got Robert shot. *You* probably want to know what happened, so I'll tell you about it.

A coroner declared Travis dead from a fatal wound to the back of his skull inflicted by a sniper from the front lawn then wheeled his lifeless body out of the house. Detective Williams and Stanford, the oddest partners that I never did see according to Paisley, took everyone's statement, except mine and Travis'. They also confiscated the recorded conversation on David's hi-tech gadget. Robert dumped my ass in an ambulance and left me in the paramedics' care to go make sure Owen never found that hit man.

He had to turn around first, come back, and then simply nod his head to the medics and cops surrounding the house. Paisley was making a scene because no one would let her ride in the ambulance with me or enter the house now surrounded by crime scene tape. Even her threats of calling her influential parents who run Miami's high society from their mayoral and district attorney posts held no sway with Miami's civil servants. That begs the question how does Robert's forehead have more power than Miami's mayor and district attorney?

I didn't seek the answer out though, instead thanking God for small favors. I didn't want to see anything that happened after I passed out. However, I wasn't spared the depressing stare of a man in his prime that had aged ten years by the time the police informed him that his son was dead and a hit man was looking for him. While I laid here, Mr. Diamond offered me several pitiful apologies for his son going off the rails. They were pitiful because he knew Travis was a highly-functioning psychotic, and turned his son loose on the world anyway without the guidance of a shrink and medication. He was hoping the structure from working in the family businesses and the influence of other sane people would keep Travis in check mentally. Make him a good man.

What Mr. Diamond got was a clever monster that wanted to take over Miami's underworld, have his father murdered just to get his inheritance of five pristine banks a little earlier so he could run dirty money through them, add them to his empire, and trap others in his web of crazy. Travis' father ended up trapped in his bank until the cops arrived to make sure no hit man was waiting for him outside. There was.

Rasheed found him before the blue shields arrived, then talked a seventeen-year-old kid from the east side with a nine millimeter in his hand out of an old beat up Chevy Impala. That kid is more than lucky that Rasheed can identify with, represent, and hopes to rescue another desperate black man caught up in the vicious cycle of survival and about to go down the drain.

Mr. Diamond finally got around to telling me about the insurance policy he found for one million dollars that I'm the beneficiary of, along with other paperwork with just Travis' signature on them. He offered me another million of hush mouth money from his pocket if I didn't speak about Travis' good or bad days to anyone. I accepted immediately. May have his grandchild in nine months. Unconditional love only provides mental and moral support. I even threw in the gift of not attending his son's funeral for free. Had no plans to stick around for it, where someone would certainly want me to speak about Travis' character. I'll tell the truth. Fortunately for them, I said goodbye to Travis in Aruba, when I learned the first true detail about his bank business.

Travis' father finally left with his broken heart, and left me alone with mine, which is what I prayed for the whole time he was talking to me. The peace and quiet didn't last long though. Paisley came back into the room, finished filling me on what else I'd missed. Blair was arrested at the Maritime Harbor on sixty counts of intent to sale and possession of stolen property worth two million dollars on the street, after he paid for what the shipment of sixty crates of narcotics. Percocet to be exact. He'd just unloaded them off the boat into his Suburban when the cops surrounded his truck intent on leaving the harbor.

That's when he learned that he was carrying one million sugar pills used in drug trials as placebos. It took Robert exactly one week to round the shipment up with Seth help's—whoever that is. Blair was singing like a bird about everyone's part in the new and upcoming Diamond Cartel before the cops could slap the handcuffs on him.

Owen and Shane caught wind of Blair's arrest and Travis' death, and they're on the run with an APB and the news crews hot on their tails. Every fifteen minutes, their wanted posters flash across every television in Miami. The low members of the Mezzane Cartel are being sought after by federal agents for thirty two cases of bank account fraud at Diamond's Banking and Trust. Mr. Diamond had just pull thirty-two suspicions accounts approved by Travis over four years. The suspiciously large weekly deposits and withdrawals caught his eye just before he found Travis' insurance policy and got the call that ruined his family. Maybe his business too, when his account holders get wind of the Pill and Banking scandal. That's what the news reporters are calling it.

None of the soldiers that opened an account at Diamond's are who their ID's say they are thanks to the meticulously criminal records kept by the FBI. That's all the American government needs to disband a major drug operation in Cuba with no low men to do the dirty work anymore. They also dabbled in flesh peddling.

I guess the rat race doesn't look so bad now to Blair, Owen, and Shane, and this is the part where I tell you what happens to me now after Operation Disturbing and my self-evaluation. I get to see a shrink for being so damn high strung from trying to maintain complete control over myself during the day. The tension and energy that I keep balled up inside of me seeks an outlet at night while I'm sleep because I won't allow it release while I'm awake. I'm a psychologist, so I know the cheapest and quickest way to get rid of it while burning the most calories is sex. Yes, it's ironic that I've been using sex for comfort just as much as Milani has but didn't know it. Doesn't make me any better than her.

Travis was actually crazy enough to like waking up to me giving him the ride of his life and what most men love more than their mama's; an orgasm. Sleep sexing won't fly with every man. Nor do I want to be disturbing other's rest. I didn't like it when Travis was doing it to mine, and will have to stop avoiding those gyms now.

I also get to be alone. Don't want just any man in my life. Now that I'm stuck on a certain someone, anyone just won't do anyway, but love and lust is truly blinding and keeps us tied to the ones that hurt us the most. I want no parts of that ever again. So as I lay here, I'm also spending time making peace with my broken heart and trying to coax it back up into my chest. While cutting the heart strings that tie me to the one that doesn't want that kind of connection to me.

There'll be at least a few unbreakable ones left. Memories of the beautiful mistakes I made with my first love are running along those threads, which is probably why we never forget your first love. Don't feel bad for me though. I've come to terms with Robert never being in my life, not looking for him to be, or hold anything against him. A man that can round up sixty crates of pharmaceutical drugs of any kind in a week has a lot of responsibility and someone to debrief about Operation Disturbing.

He's doing this world a lot of good in whatever secret job he has. This makes his inability to love me back or want a family with me completely forgivable. Now, I just need to wash the beautiful sands of

Miami off my feet and start over fresh just to get my head on straight. Well, I've been thinking about where I'll go too, and have come up with the perfect place between here and Aruba. Somewhere no one will ever think to look for me, until I'm ready to be found.

*** Two months later in Port-au-Prince, Haiti ***

It's beautiful here on the island where the first love of my life was born. I spend most of my days and nights sitting outside on the second story balcony of my property relaxing, while observing the waves roll in from the Caribbean Sea on my left. The Atlantic Ocean rushes in on my right, onto the isolated black sand beach that is all mine. It took me one month to close on the sale of the whole island with the life insurance policy that Travis left me. Another month to get an old house with great bones remodeled just the way I wanted it.

The hush-mouth million sits in Diamond's bank, collecting dust and interest along with the other three hundred grand that I've earned. I still have my business, just do conference calls with my clients and family now. That's how I was able to attend Jaden's birth in Aruba over a month and a half ago too, along with Robert. I knew he would be there, and prayed he'd ignore me completely or at least stay out of my view before I opened a window on my laptop.

A technical genius connected Milani's Skype account to the sixty-inch television in her birthing room, which gave me an in into her new life and my old one at the same time. It allowed Robert to watch me from the comfort of a brown leather chair too. He saw absolutely nothing of the baby being born right in the room with him. I kept my eyes only on Milani and Paisley, who are pissed to the highest point of pisstivity with me. I wasn't there physically to share in the baby's birth or Milani calling Rhys everything but a child of God every time a labor pain hit her.

When Jaden's head popped out with no warning, the internet signal went bad then completely out. A sudden summer rainstorm common to Haiti hit. It was depressing to be cut off from my adopted family suddenly, and relieving when the man that broke me when no other man could was gone from my view.

I know you're wondering if Milani and Paisley understand that I need to be completely alone without the added stress of trying to micromanage their lives right along with mine, while trying to coax my heart back in my chest. Absolutely! And no not really. They're my sisters by another mother who want the best for me, so I'm still here in the last place they'd think to look for me. I'm glad that they have no idea where in the hell I live, or they would be here too, micromanaging *my* life.

Being a domestic violence victim came with a perk. I didn't think I'd ever own that title in any way, or be grateful for the local program at the Miami Police Dept. that relocates women without leaving a paper trail if they want that option. All I had to do was pick a place. Unfortunately, it's almost time to tell everyone where I live. I'll have my own bundle of joy in seven months, and my family has the right to know, even if my child's father won't. Or he doesn't want to be involved. It depends on who the father is, and I don't want to do this without the people who were my rock before I ever knew I needed one.

A sudden, but often in the last couple months, downpour of melancholy descends over me and directs my attention to the middle set of three open pairs of French doors with sheer white curtains catching the evening breeze behind me. A five-disc system is mounted in the wall beside the intricately made canopy bed with white mosquito netting. There's only one song that makes me feel better.

"Sons of Funk *Pushin' Inside You*," I say loudly to the voice-activated stereo then let the melody glide over me.

It should be mental torture to listen to the song during the day then dream about Robert every night. It's not. Remember I'm different from other women in a lot of screwed up ways, and always where I want to be in my dreams; in Robert's arms without the pain that comes from wanting to be with him and can't. Every day, a little bit of that pain unfurls inside me and blows away, because living here, dreaming about Robert, and listening to our song is my way of facing my heartbreak until the dreams come no more and I get sick of Sons of Funk. Hasn't happened yet.

As soon as I settle back into my chair and the view of the lagoon below me, a door bangs shut on the first level of the house. I grasp the chair arms in a death grip then throw my feet to the rock work below them, terrified there's an intruder but going to defend my home. No one should be downstairs. My domestic help is off for the weekend. They usually lock up behind themselves. Except for two times, I haven't left the premises since a week after arriving and finding this house. Each was for a prenatal checkup.

I get up from the rocking chair that should have the imprint of my ass worn in it by now as much as I sit in it, walking slowly across the Moroccan tile floor towards the opened bedroom door. I cross over the threshold of the bedroom then tiptoe onto the balcony overlooking the great marble hall on the first floor, glancing over the solid white wood railing that circles the entire second landing. It's filled with early evening shadows. The head of a figure emerging on the staircase sends me into a defensive position. I prepare to charge forward when long dreads swing out from behind the man, but that's par for the course in Haiti.

"Finally, my psychologist," the man huffs on his way up the steps.

Not many Haitian men have wide shoulders with bulging pecs and arms with trunks for thighs that fill out khaki pants and a white Polo shirt like Robert does. No man here knows that I'm a psychologist either. All of my patients are American, domestic staff all past abused women who want nothing to do with the opposite sex.

Either my dream's come to life or Robert's walking up my stairs in the same outfit he was wearing when he flipped my world on its axis with just a touch. Well, I'm not asleep, which means he's found me somehow. However, I'm not about to let my world be flipped again. I'm just getting used to the one I built for myself.

"What are you doing here?" I yell, as he reaches the last step in his ascent.

"I'm in need of a good psychologist. Know anyone?"

His deep voice's filled with a sensual lilt hot enough to melt my core. It pools like molten lava in the pit of my stomach, where my heart still lays in the fetal position.

"I'm sure you know I'm seeing one online if you here, Robert, but you haven't answered my question."

"I told you I'm in need of a good psychologist. You."

Yeah, well, I still have issues that I'm working on, so he has to leave, and I should tell him to. Rather watch him walks toward me slowly, as if he has no cares in the world or he's making me wait for him to get closer. I shudder when I think about what could afterwards. He'll leave with the night when morning comes. Not acceptable. My heart's battered enough.

"We've established that I'm not what you want, Robert, but I can refer you to a psychologist," I whisper, missing the volume to go with the strength.

One out of two ain't bad.

When he's towering over me, the strength to make him go leaves instead.

"You're going to make this hard, aren't you?" he asks with a smile that draws my eyes to his mouth.

I clear my throat that's clogged up with emotions, then step backwards twice. "No, I'm going to say goodbye."

"Hard it is then. I love you, Trinity."

"What?" I'm not expecting my heart to jumpstart in my stomach like someone applied battery cables to it.

"From the moment I saw you in the coffee shop, woman, I knew you were going to be trouble as an adult. Yet, I couldn't stop myself from laying the ground work for making you mine one day." Then he tilts one side of his mouth up. "At least for a little while anyway until you wanted the picket fence and 2.5 kids. I knew I'd have to let you go like you have to do all precious things."

"Letting me call you by your first name was laying groundwork?" I ask condescendingly.

His grin widens. "Abso-damn-lutely! I've been Mr. Elliot to you for so long I didn't think you'd let the old bond between us go that easy to form a new one, but you did, and that was progress in my eyes." His grin fades with a thin beam of sunlight that was shining through the opened bedroom door onto the wood railing. "The next time I saw you, you were with Travis, and you were happy so I didn't lay anymore groundwork and wished you the best, until I touched you in Aruba. All bets were off. Even then, I tried to keep my distance, but I couldn't help wanting to be in your presence as much as I wanted Travis out of it. I tried to do the right thing and let you go again after we made love. I thought it was the first unselfish thing I'd done in years."

Damn! He wanted me before I even knew I wanted him.

"So why are you breaking in my house tonight?"

"Because it wasn't an unselfish thing I did. It was stupid, and I didn't have a key to let myself in, or thought you'd let me in if I knocked. Not after the way I disappeared in Miami. I'd have caught up with you in the hospital or wherever you were living if you were still there, but I learned that you'd been gone for half a day before I got back from handling some business that took longer than I thought it would."

"Business as in report to your superiors? How long have you been undercover or an informant, Robert?"

His grin comes back. "All my life it seems, and I'm undercover, all day everyday even when I quit the government agency to take Milani away from Miami. As you can see, the Bob the Builder persona follows me wherever I go. I should've quit when she was born, but the job was all I knew, how I got the chance to leave here. The adrenaline rush it gives is addicting, and sometimes you just forget who you really are. I should've known you'd figure it out though, even when no one else has. What I do is dangerous, Trinity. I can't tell you the name of the agency I work for because it doesn't exist, but families pay the price regularly for what I do."

Strangely, I don't need all the answers anymore, just one. "Doesn't explain why you're here."

"I wouldn't be here if you weren't. Almost everything I want by my side is here standing in front of me where it all began when I was given a choice to get my shit together at eighteen or do hard time for almost killing a rival drug lord that was being hunted by a man that shall remain nameless and now runs the agency." Yeah, that would probably be Seth.

"Robert, I'm pregnant and I don't know who the father is," I blurt out, and I have got to stop doing that.

"Me," he deadpans.

"You don't know—"

"If it's yours, it's mine. We didn't use protection, so I have no reason to get mad or judge you for not knowing who the father is. I knew you had a man when I came on to you subtly. That makes me trifling, doesn't it?"

"If it does, it makes me trifling too, Robert. I knew I had a man as well, but Travis, who was definitely trifling caught me asleep and took advantage. I want this child, so I'm not getting rid of it no matter who's the father. Do you understand why we can't be together?" I won't even bring up my issue of straddling men in the night and having my way with them.

"No, and I'm not leaving one more child's life that I'm supposed to be a part of. If I wasn't, you wouldn't have made love to me."

"I have no problem with you being a part of its life." I do, but I'll deal with it... head on.

"What about me being a part of your life, Trinity?"

"Truthfully, I'm skittish of you right now. You hurt me badly, Robert."

"I know and I'm so damn sorry, sweetheart, but I didn't expect to find a scaredy-cat after you tried to protect me with your life. No braver thing can be done."

Except risk my heart again.

"You weren't supposed to die like that, but my broken heart's not the worst part. Apparently, I'm dangerous to men, so you should think twice about wanting to be near me for any length of time."

He lifts both eyebrows and crosses his arms over his chest before spreading his feet part. "I'm not supposed to be without the woman that I love either. Now how dangerous?"

"I'm such a control freak pressure to be the best walls up inside of me. My body releases it in the only way it knows how when I'm sleep... by straddling a man and riding him until we both cum."

He starts to chuckle, and his hilarity grows in volume until he's laughing his ass off. "And someone told you there was something dangerous about that? Either you need a new psychologist, or another man that'll help you release the excess stress *before* you go to sleep, Trinity."

"That's what my psychologist said after it occurred to us both that my sleep sexing started when Travis cut me off during the weekends when I could release the pent up energy. I started taking what I wanted from him without knowing I was doing it because he was feeding my need for perfection with his lifestyle but not giving me what I needed the most while I was awake... but I always knew he wasn't the man for me. I'd chosen Travis because he couldn't hurt me emotionally."

Robert huffs. "Of course he wasn't the right man. I'm right here." Then he smiles down at me. "Sleep sexing, huh? I like the sound of that and want to try it sometimes."

"Oh hell nawl!" Milani's yell drifts in from the open balcony all the way onto the veranda." Everybody, let's go back to the hotel! Trinity can meet Jaden tomorrow."

My head turns in the direction of the balcony.

"Just wait a minute, Milani," Paisley starts, but her voice wanes before I can hear whatever rants she's about to go off on.

It probably has to do a lot with the interrupting of her eavesdropping on my conversation.

"You brought them too!" I screech like a damn girl.

"The whole crew. We were worried about you isolating yourself in Haiti after Travis' death. We tried to give you some space to come to what you already know; nothing that happened is your fault. After two months, we're over the waiting, and came to make sure you're okay."

He walks closer.

I stop breathing. "You knew where I was this whole time?"

He nods. "My job gives me connections to everything that deals with the government and whatever's below that. You were still on the plane when I found you. There's always a trail, Trinity. I shouldn't have let you go anywhere after Aruba, but my job to take down drug dealers already established and up and coming was too easy to fall back into it. Old habits die hard, and sometimes our targets' families exact revenge on the families of the men who bring them down. I couldn't live if something happened to someone I love, so it became second nature to be single, but my daughter needed me. Now, I need you.

I rather teach you combat skills more effective than your wild woman technique that took Travis by surprise, but the element of surprise only lasts so long as you found out. You may need to actually save you baby's daddy's life one day instead of getting in the way of a sniper who was supposed to take the head shot if I couldn't bring Travis out alive. He almost didn't get the shot anyway because he was laughing his night-goggle wearing ass off at you bomb rushing a man and screaming your head off while doing it. The sniper was Albert by the way. He's put in a request to meet you personally."

I start to laugh hysterically. "Sorry, I didn't know you guys had a plan and you were the decoy that would draw Travis in front of the window. All I knew was he wasn't going to shoot you again."

"That sounds like love to me, and I'd be a fool to let it get away again. So tell me Trinity, have I given you any reason to take me back yet? Or do I need to grovel on my knees or take another bullet for you for being stupid in thinking I could live without the woman I should've taken as mine four years ago?"

"I don't know," I tease, then walk right up to his chest after hearing what I've being waiting on. His words echo in every battered chamber of my heart, but I haven't heard everything I need to yet. "You told me you didn't want kids and marriage, and we were never really together."

"Sweetheart, we were together when you unsnapped your dress in Aruba. I lied about wanting kids and marriage with you, but I screwed up the first time with Jessica and Milani. That's a hard pill to swallow for a man who can run a criminal empire and enough legit companies to be considered for a Fortune 500 expo while undercover."

"Sometimes, we don't get everything right the first time, Robert."

"Then stand beside me and guide me through the second time. Be my everything and I'll be yours to the best of my abilities."

My everything is finally mine. "Who told you what to say to me?"

"Me!" Milani yells up the balcony.

"You weren't the only one, Milani," Paisley pipes in.

Deep laughter indicative of eavesdropping men standing below the balcony too rang out. I shake my head.

"You cheated, Robert," I mention casually, as his hands swing for then land on my hips.

The tingle that isn't so shocking anymore but just as powerful fires off under my skin, followed by the customary shiver down my spine and goose bumps on my arms.

"All's fair in love and justice, sweetheart."

"If you still want to work undercover, I can wait for you. That's all my heart's been doing anyway."

"Not necessary. I'm officially out of work. I missed Milani's birth while waiting for an idiot dealer to find his way out of his own state, my first failure to my family. I'm not missing another child's birth or breaking your heart again. Neither of us has to work again. Haven't you heard? I'm worth millions."

"So am I, well, I'm worth *a* million anyway, and I like working."

My hands glide around his neck of their own free will. I don't mind my body doing its own thing with this man.

"Then by all means, work, Trinity, and I'll be chief, cook, and bottle washer."

"What if the baby is—"

"Mine! Both of you are," he growls. "And you owe me something."

"I love you, Robert," I say softly.

He smiles then plants his lips on mine. I fall prey to them, giving them everything they want from me willingly, which is everything, including my heart that settled back in my chest as soon as his lips touched mine. And then, his are gone. I whimper into his neck. At least his arms are still holding me.

"I love you too, Trinity, and as your man, it's my duty to warn you of things incoming."

No, no, no, no more gates to hell opening on this family, but I know with life, shit happens.

"What is it this time, Robert?"

"It's Paisley. Her parents are coming after Rasheed."

"Yeah, I knew that would happen eventually. They're neurotic when it comes to Paisley's future husband. He doesn't fit the qualifications. Does she know what they're up to?"

"Why do you think I'm telling you? She doesn't know because she won't answer her phone."

"And I have to play messenger. What do I need to do for her?"

"What you've always done: be there for her. She's going to need you. What *we* are going to do together, love, is protect our people."

"I like the sound of 'we'."

"It's permanent."

Hopefully, the storm kicking up on the edges of Paisley's world isn't.

THE END... for now.

Find out who fathered Trinity's child in Paisley's Story.

Stay updated by following London Starr on these sites.

Facebook Like Page

Amazon Author Page

Interact with me here:
https://www.facebook.com/groups/londonandtheresa/

Thank you for supporting this work. I truly hoped you enjoyed it. Definitely, leave a review if you feel up to it. If not, I more than appreciate you just letting me entertain you. It is a privilege that I hope to access again and again in the future. For updates on London Starr's latest releases not promoted in this work, click these links and follow me on social media and Amazon. I follow back. Have a beautiful life and excellent reads always at your fingertips.

ABOUT THE AUTHOR

London Starr's a full-time mother of three girls, wife, and author pursuing a lifelong dream of writing thrillers, often interracial, some urban fiction and paranormal. She's received an award in the 2015 IR Author Swirl in Best Paranormal Romance category for her first self-published novel, Ileeria: The Chosen One, before being selected as a judge for the 5th annual IR Author Swirl Awards.

Griffin, Georgia's her home, where she developed the passion for reading, writing, and sharing her imagination, but not where she was born. She hopes to travel through her hometown in Kansas as an adult and sponsor shelters for domestic abuse victims throughout the USA. Until then, nothing makes her happier than to raise her family, start a book, and then complete it, whether she's reading someone else's work or writing her own.

Available

Milani's Story: The Trifling Series 1

A beautiful woman decides to turn her life around just before her bad acts come back to haunt her.
#crime #romance

http://bit.ly/Trifling1

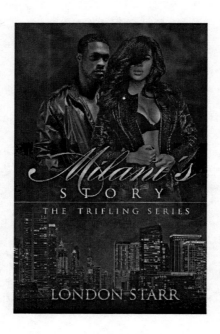

Available

Work, Play Kill

A killer with two faces, and a detective that he
hides both sides of him from.
#crime #romance

http://bit.ly/WorkPlayKillebook

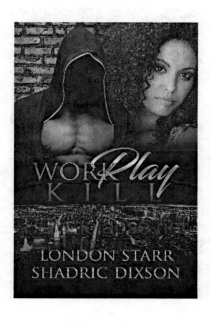

Available

A Kingpin's Obsession: Ajoni's Story

When love finds a drug lord who's used to taking what he wants.
#urban #romance

http://amzn.to/1S5NxW7

Available

The Ink Masters': Gangster Desires

#urban collaboration
1. A Kingpin's Obsession 2: Chiness' Story by London Starr
#urban #romance
2. Carolina Shot Caller by Honey Bee.
#urban #crime

http://bit.ly/GangsterDesireebook

Available

The Ink Masters': Book of the Unknown

#sci fi collaboration
1. Alien Siege by London Starr
#romance
2. The Beast Within Me by Honey Bee.
#urban

http://bit.ly/2inkmastersBOTU

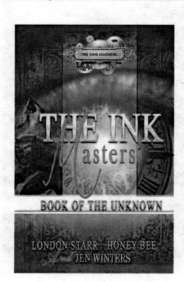

Available

Undisclosed Desire

Powerful men who will learn rarely do love and money go hand in hand. #bwwm #romance

http://bit.ly/undisclosed1

Coming 8/1

My Mother's Footsteps

When family becomes one woman's salvation and her downfall.
#crime #romance

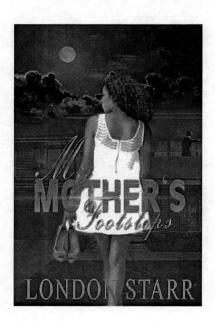

Coming 10/2

Slader Falls:
Female Shifters, Human Mates 1

A new spin on paranormal that centers around
female shifters and their firefighting mates.
#romance #paranormal

CPSIA information can be obtained
at www.ICGtesting.com
Printed in the USA
LVOW10s1943190418
574122LV00013B/863/P